THE DUTIFUL DOCTOR

THE DUTIFUL DOCTOR

Claire Vernon

Chivers Press   •   **Thorndike Press**
Bath, England   **Waterville, Maine USA**

This Large Print edition is published by Chivers Press, England, and by Thorndike Press, USA.

Published in 2002 in the U.K. by arrangement with the author's estate.

Published in 2002 in the U.S. by arrangement with Juliet Burton Literary Agency.

U.K. Hardcover   ISBN 0–7540–4929–9 (Chivers Large Print)
U.K. Softcover   ISBN 0–7540–4930–2 (Camden Large Print)
U.S. Softcover   ISBN 0–7862–4252–3 (Nightingale Series Edition)

The text of this Large Print edition is unabridged.
Other aspects of the book may vary from the original edition.

Set in 16 pt. New Times Roman.

Printed in Great Britain on acid-free paper.

British Library Cataloguing in Publication Data available

Library of Congress Cataloging-in-Publication Data

Vernon, Claire.
　　The dutiful doctor / by Claire Vernon.
　　　　p.　　cm.
　　ISBN 0–7862–4252–3 (lg. print : sc : alk. paper)
　　1. Young women—Fiction. 2. Orphans—Fiction. 3. Twins—
Fiction. 4. Large type books. I. Title.
PR6072.E735 D88 2002
823'.914—dc21　　　　　　　　　　　　　　　　2002024153

CHAPTER ONE

Adam Bray was locking his suitcase when the inter-com phone bell rang. Frowning slightly, he answered it. A tall, lean man with light brown hair, brown eyes and a quiet face. A strange way to describe it, perhaps, but when he smiled, his whole face came to life, his eyes sparkled, his rather disciplined mouth relaxed.

It was Rhoda, the nurse receptionist in her reception-office on the ground floor, speaking.

'I'm sorry to bother you, Dr. Bray,' she said in her lilting voice. 'But I can't get hold of either of the doctors and . . .'

'Rhoda, I told you I'm flying up to Amanzi this morning and . . .'

'I know, Doctor, and I'm sorry to have to trouble you but Sister Ann sounded real upset and she isn't one to panic . . .' Rhoda said apologetically.

'Sister Ann. No, you're right. It must be urgent. Know what it's about?'

'That little girl, Christine, I think her name is. The . . .'

'I know. She's being operated on tomorrow and being moved from St. Christopher's today. Look, Rhoda, tell Emmanuel to come round right away with the car. He can wait for me at the Clinic and then take me to the airport. I'll phone you later and will you give the message

1

immediately to Dr. Fox when he comes in?'

'Of course, Doctor . . . and . . . and might I say how sorry I am to hear about your father. Is it very bad?'

'Frankly I don't know but I'm afraid so. I've seen this developing for some time. He's no chicken, you know. Going on sixty-nine yet expects to be able to caper about like a sixteen-year-old. Sometimes I think he's never grown up.'

'But that must be fine, Doctor. To feel so young, I mean. Better than feeling old before your time . . .'

Adam laughed. Rhoda was just twenty years old and constantly telling them that she was now one of the 'oldies'.

'Yes, I rather envy him,' Adam admitted. 'But it's tough on those who worry about him. You'll send for Emmanuel at once?'

'Of course, Doctor . . .' Rhoda rang off and Adam replaced the receiver.

He went to the window, drew up the venetian blinds he detested with a vicious tug, and stared out. His bedroom and study was on the eighth floor and he had a good view of Durban's harbour with the big white liners in the docks and the scurrying crowd of people on their way to work. He wondered if it was worth trying to get through on the phone to Amanzi. Had they had time to mend the fallen telephone wires? He'd phoned the night before as soon as he got the telegram but he'd been told that the district in which his parents lived, was out of order owing to a severe thunderstorm. So he'd sent a wire saying he was flying up. If only his car hadn't been backed into by that stupid fool of a woman learner . . . if . . .

He looked round the room. How he hated the avant-garde way—which was how Marie Fox described it—in which it was designed. The glaring colours that fought for predominance, the modern furniture that didn't invite you to sit down and relax. He sighed. There were so many matters in which he and Marie failed to see eye to eye, he thought, with a rueful smile. Marie was the only child of the senior partner of the small group of doctors to which Adam belonged. A very lovely girl but determined to marry him. Only Adam was equally determined not to marry her! How many times had you to tell a girl that you didn't love her or intend to marry her? Did she expect him to write it down on paper, carefully dotting his 'i's' and crossing his 't's'?

With his usual methodical tidiness, he checked that he had forgotten nothing, then took his raincoat—for summer was the rainy season in Amanzi—from the wardrobe and put it over his arm, and lifted his suitcase. He went from the room to the silent lift that hardly seemed to move but dropped him to the ground floor. At least, he'd already said goodbye to Marie. A wild tornado-like farewell in which she lost her temper and accused him of being a 'weakling', a 'mother's pet' and a 'coward'. He had remained quiet throughout the quarrel, another thing which always riled Marie for she liked both to quarrel and then have an emotional scene of forgiveness.

'I don't believe your father is ill . . .' she had raged, her small slender body shaking with anger. 'This is just a ploy of your mother's, a way of getting you up there for Christmas.'

'Mother's been a doctor's wife for nearly thirty years,' Adam had said quietly. 'She wouldn't do a thing like that.'

'Oh yes she would. She's possessive. She resents me. She's afraid I'll steal you from her . . . this is just a mean . . .'

'Please, Marie . . .' Adam had tried to calm her. 'I've been expecting this for some time. Dad's whole behaviour has pointed to this. It's simply that it's come a few years sooner than I thought it would.'

'How long will you have to stay?' Marie had flung the question as she might have thrown a dagger.

He'd shrugged. 'How can I tell?'

'And what did Dad say when you told him you were calmly walking out?'

'He understood I had no choice.'

'But you have a choice . . .' Marie had come to stand close to him. He could smell the

4

expensive perfume she used. He knew she expected him to put his arms around her but he had no wish to do so. 'Adam . . .' Marie had gone on, her voice soft and beguiling. 'You have a choice. You're a man. You're thirty and your whole future is involved. Dad thinks a lot of you, Adam, but if you just go off every time your mother sends for you . . . well, you're not exactly reliable, are you?' She had gazed up at him appealingly. She was a bit of a girl, just over five feet tall, and beautiful. 'Adam, I have faith in you,' she went on softly. 'One day you'll be a great doctor. But burying yourself in that dump won't help you. Dad can help you . . . so can I . . .'

Somehow he had got away. Adam could remember Marie's tears and wondering, in his cold unromantic way if she kept a bit of cut onion in her hankie to bring the tears at the right moment! What always amazed him—for he'd seen a lot of women in tears in the course of his work—was how beautiful Marie remained even while she wept.

Now as he walked out of the big block of offices and flats to the black Chevrolet waiting for him, he realised his biggest mistake had been in agreeing to live with the Foxes. Mrs. Fox had been very friendly, had said he'd be no trouble and it would be helpful to have him 'on the spot', Gerald Fox had agreed, said they had two spare rooms, but Adam knew that, if only he'd had the sense to realise it then, it was

Marie's idea! Now what was there about him that attracted a girl like Marie? he wondered. No one had ever called him good-looking. He had a biggish nose, was already showing signs that one day he'd be bald, had very ordinary hair, he wasn't a good dancer, he loathed social 'do's'. In fact he loathed all the things Marie loved and she loathed everything that he thought made life worth living. Maybe it was because he was hard to get, he thought with a rueful smile, as Emmanuel smiled with a big grin and slid behind the steering wheel.

'St. Christopher's please, Emmanuel . . .'

The sun was already very hot, promising another sweltering day of humidity but Adam would, in an hour, be high up in the air, speeding back towards Amanzi and the mountains.

Adam relaxed, leaning back, folding his arms, as Emmanuel wove his way through the busy traffic. Maybe with Adam out of the way, Marie would forget him, he thought. It was difficult to cope with the situation without being brutal, but it was beginning to get embarrassing. He'd seen Rhoda's smile as she passed on an 'urgent message' from Marie— Nick and Josh, two of the other junior partners, had teased him about 'hanging up his hat in the hall' and being 'the clever one'.

The big black car drew up outside the white building.

'I shouldn't be long, Emmanuel.' Adam

6

glanced at his wristwatch. 'I've got to be at the airport in three-quarters of an hour . . .'

'We'll make it,' Emmanuel promised.

Adam walked into the cool quiet building from the hot humid air. He smiled at the girl in the reception office and went up in the lift to the third floor of the Clinic.

St. Christopher's Clinic was renowned for its good staff and pleasant atmosphere. Run by nuns, Adam and the rest of the doctors he worked with, went there voluntarily. Now as he passed the glass doors of the wards, he glanced in casually, smiling if he recognised one of the smooth-moving nuns, until he reached the Children's Ward.

Sister Antoinette came hurrying. 'Sister Ann asked me to explain, Doctor. Christine is very upset, she says she wants to stay here, that people die when they go to Carnavon Hospital . . . If you look at her chart . . .'

'I will, Sister, thank you . . .' Adam said a little curtly as he hurried down the aisle between the beds of children, many of whom waved at him or called out. He saw Christine long before he reached her. She was sobbing hysterically, clinging to a young woman who held her close, one hand stroking Christine's long fair hair. Christine was barely nine years old but she had a will of her own.

'I won't go . . . I won't go . . .' Christine was sobbing. 'I'll die if I go there. St. Christopher's my guardian angel. I've got to stay . . .'

7

Adam picked up the chart, his eyebrows nearly meeting as he read what was written there. He turned to the Sister by his side.

'I'd like to check . . .'

'Of course, Doctor . . .' The heavily-built nun who moved with such surprising lightness, bent over the sobbing child and murmured something to the young woman who reluctantly let go of Christine and stood up.

Adam barely glanced at her. He was thinking fast . . . but he did vaguely notice how unfashionably long the young woman's navy blue dress was and how her dark hair was braided round her head. She stood up, eyes demurely cast down and stood back but as he casually glanced at her, she lifted her head and stared at him. She was tall. Nearly as tall as he was, he noted vaguely, but suddenly her dark eyes were alive—alive with anguish, warm with pleading.

'Please, Doctor . . .' she almost whispered. 'Couldn't the operation be done here? It means so much to Christine . . .'

'Charon . . .' Sister Antoinette was saying in a shocked voice.

But Adam nodded. 'I'll see what can be done,' he promised, bent down over the hysterical child and forgot everything else.

CHAPTER TWO

Charon Webb went quietly down the ward, smiling and waving to the children in the beds. She knew the nuns preferred her to visit the ward during the quiet afternoons and she had only come to see Christine because she heard the child was so upset.

Poor Christine, who had spent most of her life in hospitals, shuttled from one to the other so that she rarely stayed for more than a few months in each place. Here she had been her longest—for eight whole months, and it was the nearest approach to home the child had ever had. She also wore a St. Christopher's medallion round her neck and was convinced he was her guardian angel and that no harm could come to her while under his care. This operation was to do with Christine's brain, but they did sometimes do brain operations here, so why was the poor little kid to be carted off somewhere where she would know no one, recognise no familiar face?

As Charon went running down the stairs to the ground floor and out into the hot sunshine, she told herself that everything would be all right. He had said he'd do his best. What were the words he'd used? She tried to remember. Oh, yes, 'I'll see what I can do.'

Dr. Adam Bray was liked by all the nuns in

9

the Clinic. They thought more highly of him than of any of the other doctors, despite his youth.

'He has time for people,' Sister Ann had once said.

'He really cares . . .' was what Sister Mary told Charon.

'He cares too much,' the Mother Superior had said. Charon had been surprised but was too well-trained to ask what the Mother Superior meant.

Now as she crossed the quadrangle and went to the tall grey building that was her home and the Convent's Hostel, Charon reminded herself that this was an important day.

December 8th.

And her nineteenth birthday!

As she turned into the rather cheerless, spotlessly clean hostel, she glanced up at the letter rack.

One letter for Miss Charon Webb.

Before she opened the envelope she knew who it was from. There was only one person in the whole world who ever wrote to her.

Mrs. Jugg! Dear old Mrs. Jugg!

It was a birthday card. A pretty one of red roses and golden mimosa and Mrs. Jugg had written in her hard-to-read scrawly writing:

'Happy birthday, dear child, and may those birthdays that are to come be happier than the ones you've already had.'

For a moment, Charon's eyes smarted as she turned and climbed two flights of uncarpeted stairs. Mrs. Jugg always understood.

Sixty years and a bit old, Mrs. Jugg had worked hard all her life, carefully saving. Now she had a small cottage at Isipingo and lived there with her small Peke dog and a canary. But regularly twice a week, she made the journey into Durban to visit the Clinic and the orphanage and to spread what she called 'a little cheer'. For Mrs. Jugg had been an orphan herself at St. Christopher's and knew very well what it felt like.

Not that life was bad at St. Christopher's, Charon thought with a quick feeling of guilt. They had been more than kind to her. She'd had a good education—even if she'd not made much use of it— led a good life but . . .

There was always that little 'but'.

In an orphanage, you were always one of a crowd. Never just 'the' one, the important one to someone. That was what she had missed. When her parents had died, she'd been eight years old. Would she ever forget that day? she wondered.

Now as she unlocked the door of her room, she looked round her. This was her home.

This small bleak room with its white walls, dark blue curtains and matching bedspread. The chest of drawers. The small mirror on the wall. The only warm human thing in the room

11

was the photograph.

Now she went and picked it up, her sorrow welling up again in her throat. She loved her parents so much. So very very much.

How young they looked! But then they could only have been in their mid-thirties. A coloured photo, showing her mother's red hair and her father's brown. Funny that her hair was so black. It must be from her grandparents whom she'd never known. There'd just been the three of them. Dad, Mum and herself. And she was often ill but they'd understood, and been patient with her. What lovely holidays they'd had. Up in the Drakensbergs. Once they'd gone down to the Cape. And then there'd come that day when she'd hurried home from school. It was half past three and she had been surprised to find the front door locked. It had been a hot day like this . . .

Charon held the photograph to her and jerked a chair close to the open window. The only view was of the shining windows of the big Clinic but she was not looking at it, she had retreated eleven years to the day she went home and the house was empty.

She'd walked round to the back but the kitchen door was locked so she'd shouted for Martha and she came running down the pathway, her dark face sleepy, her eyes half closed.

'Mummy and Dad said they'd be home,' Charon had said accusingly.

Martha had blinked. 'Maybe lots of cars on the road.'

The house was still empty at seven o'clock that night, Charon and Martha sitting very quietly. Martha in the kitchen, the dinner bubbling on the Aga, Charon curled up on the window sill watching the road.

She'd been startled when she saw a policeman walking to the front door, and with the policeman was . . . a nun.

And then everything seemed to have gone haywire. Charon had refused to believe it. God couldn't be so cruel.

'God loves us,' she'd sobbed to the nun, 'so he wouldn't take Mummy and Daddy from me.'

The nun had been kind. 'Perhaps God needs your Mummy and Daddy.'

'He can't. He's got everything and I've got nothing . . .' Charon had wailed. 'I need my Mummy and Daddy . . .'

But the tears had been no good. God hadn't sent back her Mummy and Daddy. Instead she had gone to live at St. Christopher's.

Oh, they'd been kindness itself. So had the other girls. All sorry for her but pointing out that she'd been lucky to have her parents that long. Many of them were orphans from soon after birth. But there'd always been a vacuum in Charon's life. An emptiness. And Mrs. Jugg had done her best to fill that emptiness. On her visits, she had spent most of her time talking to Charon. Later, she'd been allowed to have Charon out for the day. She'd given Charon presents. Hand-made gifts, but she'd give her something far more important—the feeling of belonging to someone.

Charon Webb . . . nineteen, without a relative in the world. So far as she knew, Charon thought. It gave her a strange feeling, as if she was floating in space, drifting, attached to nothing and no one. Just a very small piece of life in an enormous indifferent world.

She had few friends. She found it hard to make friends, somehow, for always there was the fear of growing too fond of someone and of losing that person. One day Mrs. Jugg would be very old and die and then there would be no one.

It was unusual for Charon to sit and indulge in self-pity. She'd been brought up to despise it. To know that the only way to cope with problems is to face up to them. But this was a problem she felt unable to solve.

How did you stop being a nothing? For that was all you were when you belonged to no one and no one belonged to you.

This was her home. Mother Superior had wanted her to get a job in Durban, to live in another hostel, meet a fresh lot of girls but she had begged to stay on. She knew this place, the faces. Somehow she felt safe here. Sometimes she went into town to shop but always she had hurried back, unable to understand the fear that had filled her as she walked the streets alone.

Of course a lot of it was, she knew, lack of self-confidence. She was so tall, much taller than any of the other girls. And lanky. She had long legs, too. And was clumsy, always falling over things. Nor did she find it easy to make conversation. She had tried. She'd tried very hard. But she invariably ended up by saying: 'Really?' 'Yes, I know.' 'I see . . .' Nothing very intelligent, or helpful towards continuing a difficult conversation. What was there to talk about, in any case? The Hostel, the Clinic, the Nursery School where she worked? What outsider would be interested in that? What insider, either, for that matter. Sometimes she wanted to scream: If only something could happen! Yet she knew very well that if it did happen, she would be the first to run away as fast as she could because she'd be scared to death.

What was she going to do with her life? It was a question that bothered her. She'd an idea that old Mrs. Jugg had left the cottage to her so she'd have that, at least. Perhaps she could start a Nursery School in Isipingo . . . but that was no good. She had only trained as an Assistant. But she couldn't just stay here all the days of her life teaching pre-school children. Or could she? Or wasn't it perhaps more correct to ask: would she!

Nineteen-years-old, and she was already in a rut. In a safe, boringly dull, miserably lonely little rut. Why hadn't she the courage to break out of it? The Mother Superior would help her willingly.

'You mustn't depend on us, dear child,' she'd said once. 'In life you walk alone—but remember, God is always with you.'

Charon had never quite forgiven God for having taken away her parents though she knew this was wrong of her, and she often prayed to be able to understand why He had done such a thing. Most of her religious life at St. Christopher's had been difficult for she was divided between what she wanted to believe and what she did believe. She had never been able to explain this to anyone; indeed, it was something she was very ashamed about.

She jumped as someone knocked on the door and opened it at the same time.

Netta Walk stood there, her fair hair neatly braided round her head, her face anxious.

'Charon, Mother Superior wants to see you. Are you in some sort of trouble?'

Netta was a real gossip and she loved to make the worst of everything, Charon knew.

She stood up, putting the photograph down. 'Not that I know of . . .' she said. She went to the mirror to make sure her hair was tidy. She straightened the slightly crumpled skirt of her dark blue cotton frock.

'Well, I couldn't help wondering,' Netta

16

said, giving her a strange look. 'You see, there's a young man in there with her.'

Charon looked startled. 'A young man? What on earth could a young man have to do with me? I don't even know one—apart from those who sing in the choir and come to the youth club.'

'Oh it isn't a young man like that, Charon. This one's wealthy. Got a grand sports car. Smartly dressed, too.' Netta's eyes were sparkling. She'd have something to tell the other girls at lunch, Charon thought, feeling rather amused.

And then she grew a bit worried. It was unlike the Mother Superior to send for one of her staff on a Saturday morning. This was the day that the Canon always called and stayed for lunch. So it must be about something important.

'You'd better hurry,' Netta said eagerly. 'She's a bit annoyed already. Cheeks all red and hot as if she was upset about something . . .'

'I can't think what about . . .' Charon said and hurried away.

CHAPTER THREE

The plane circled and landed perfectly, with the merest hint of a bump. Adam could see his mother waiting patiently. He stood and stretched himself. He was not particularly fond of flying and would have preferred to have driven up through the night but unfortunately his car would not be ready for another two weeks, at least.

His mother waved as he went down the steps to the ground and it was not long before he was by her side.

'Dear Adam,' she said, hugging him warmly. 'Bless you for coming so quickly. Was it difficult?'

She was a short woman, inclined towards plumpness but her life was too full to worry much about her appearance. He had often thought she was one of the happiest women he knew. And wondered why, for life with the old doctor couldn't always have been honey. Her white hair was cut short, her clothes considered eccentric but the plain truth was that she was not interested either in clothes or her looks. There were too many other things to think about. She just loved 'people', sitting on committees, doing everything she could to help others less fortunate than herself. She loved her garden and worked hard in it, wrote reams of letters which were rarely answered, and—like the old-fashioned toy that always came up again when knocked down—she never let anything worry or upset her.

'No, it wasn't too difficult,' Adam told her reassuringly. 'Dr. Fox understood.'

His mother's blue eyes twinkled. 'But Marie didn't?'

'No but then, Marie never does like anything I do. Don't let's talk of her. I've had a . . .'

His mother chuckled. 'Is she chasing you? I can imagine it. Poor Marie.'

'Poor Marie?' Adam pretended to be shocked. 'What about poor me?'

'You can take it but she can't. I expect it's the first time she's been refused anything.'

They walked to where the car was parked. The same old red car.

'How's Dad?'

'Furious with me for sending for you. He says I'm an old fuss-pot, that he's a hundred per cent fit and . . .'

'And is he?'

She looked up at him. 'He blacked out four times yesterday,' she said simply. 'You drive, Adam.' She got into the car. 'Once as he walked into the hospital . . . once as he got out of the car at home . . . once in the garden and . . . and once last night. That's why I wired you. I felt that it shouldn't be ignored.'

'You were quite right,' Adam told her as he

19

slid behind the steering wheel and began to drive. 'Looks like you had a lot of rain . . .'

'Two inches yesterday. Terrific storm, too. Most of the phones are out of order.'

'I know. I tried to ring you . . .'

'I thought you'd drive up.'

'I would have but some crazy woman driver who was driving a L marked car, reversed into mine and did quite a bit of damage. The insurance covers it but it's the darned nuisance of being without a car . . .'

'Well, you'll have this. I've told your father he's not to drive.'

Adam chuckled. 'I bet he was mad.'

His mother laughed. 'He was, too! However, I pointed out that if he blacked out while driving he could kill some innocent child. That floored him, bless him.' Her smile, Adam saw as he glanced down at her, was tender. 'He's going to hate this, Adam,' she added.

'I know.'

Adam concentrated on his driving. He'd been two years now in Durban and was unused to earth roads that were thick with mud. The car skidded slightly as the road began to climb, leaving the valley behind. Glancing sideways, he saw the new hospital. White, imposing, very modern as it sat on the hillside, overlooking the valley and the small town of Ukoma.

'Looks good . . .'

His mother laughed. 'It's still inadequate, according to your Dad. He fought bitterly for a separate T.B. building and a Leprosarium but most of the folk think these should be right out of town . . .'

Adam nodded. 'Still scared of them. Funny. You can try to educate the man in the street but some of these deep-rooted fears are impossible to overcome. I wonder how many people appreciate the fact that today, a man with leprosy can be treated safely at home and with no fear of spreading the disease. We have means of determining . . .'

Rose Bray sat back in the car, hands folded, body relaxed, as she listened to Adam 'up on his soap box', as he called it himself. It was good to have the boy home. Henry was a difficult man to handle and he was going to hate being dependent. Obstinate, stubborn, poor love. It wasn't going to be easy for any of them. She wished Adam would be more frank with her. Just how ill was Henry, she wondered.

They were driving past the Lillingtons' farm now. Sam was a good farmer. The citrus trees looked good. Suddenly she felt she couldn't bear the suspense and she put her hand lightly in Adam's arm.

'I must know, Adam, just how bad is it?'

She saw the way he hesitated and her fingers tightened round his arm.

'Please don't lie to me, darling. I can take the truth better than a half-truth.'

He nodded, turning off the main road and

going down the narrow track that led to their house.

'It could be very bad,' he said curtly. 'It could also be very little. I talked to Dr. Fox and he told me of some tests I can make without Dad knowing it. He says we must get him to a specialist. He . . .'

'Takes a dim view?'

'I wouldn't say that but he's not unduly optimistic. He says Dad must go down to Durban and have a proper examination. If we can do that, he reckons Dad stands a good chance . . .'

' "If" being the operative word,' his mother said dryly.

'Exactly. Don't worry. Leave it to me,' Adam said, hoping he sounded more optimistic than he felt. His father wasn't going to be easy to handle!

Now as they came in sight of the single-storied, long white house with its wide step, he saw the old man was sitting out there. Smoking, of course! And with a glass of whisky on the table beside him! Would he never learn, Adam wondered. Perhaps he didn't want to, perhaps life so constricted was not life as he wanted it.

'The garden's looking fine,' Adam said and saw his mother glow with pride.

'It isn't being an easy summer,' she said. 'First the rains came late, then they came too heavy. Yesterday's storm didn't help matters.'

'Still looks pretty good to me,' he said as he drew up outside the carport, looking at the purple bougainvillaea that climbed up the end of the house, at the wide bed of white and pink stocks, at the roses in flower, and already a few of her precious dahlias, big golden blooms.

As he lifted his case out of the car, Absalom came running in his white jacket and shorts, his dark face bright with welcome, grabbing the suitcase, putting it on his shoulder and marching indoors.

Adam drew a long deep breath and looked at the mountains round them. The house had been built in a good position. Half-way up a mountain, gazing over the valley, with mountains in the distance, a strange blue colour. He could see the citrus farms on the mountainside, their trees marching in ballet-like symmetry, beautiful in their neat precision. Then he followed his mother up the two steps to the stoep.

Henry Bray stood up slowly. He was a tall man, too thin, really, but it was not surprising for he was rarely still. He was bald except for a few wisps of hair, his eyes sunken, deep lines between his nose and chin.

'This is utterly ridiculous . . .' he began angrily. And then keeled over.

Adam caught him before he hit the ground. He was shocked to realise how thin the old man was for he hardly weighed anything. Absalom was there to help and as they laid the old man on his bed, Absalom's dark eyes met Adam's.

'Is the old Master very sick?' he asked.

Adam shrugged. 'I don't know but I . . .'

Absalom nodded wisely. 'He will not agree . . .'

Adam smiled. 'I know . . .'

He waited by the bedside until Henry Bray opened his eyes. The old man blinked, looked round as if surprised, and then turned to look at Adam.

He gave a rather rueful smile. 'Not a very good welcome, son, but maybe I should say, touché. I can get up?'

The question made Adam turn away hastily. It was an admission the old boy had made. He was in Adam's hands. That meant he knew.

CHAPTER FOUR

Charon knocked on the door and heard the voice of the Mother Superior. A little scared, and very curious as to the reason of this unusual summons on a Saturday morning, Charon went in.

Mother Superior was sitting behind her desk. Her tranquil face flushed, her eyes worried and unhappy.

'Come in, Charon,' she repeated.

It was then Charon saw the man Netta had

24

mentioned. A tall man with broad shoulders and longish dark hair, dark eyes. A face that seemed strangely familiar. Yet she had never seen him before. He was quite unlike any of the men she had met. As Netta had said, he was different. His clothes looked expensive, he looked . . . well, different!

He took a step forward, his hand out, his voice eager. 'It must be . . .'

The Mother Superior lifted her hand. 'Please, Mr. Mortlake,' she said sternly. 'You promised to let me handle this.'

His hand dropped to his side, and his face clouded.

'I'm sorry.'

'Charon, let me introduce Mr. Mortlake. Mr. Mortlake, this is Charon Webb,' Mother Superior said formally.

Charon looked at him quickly and saw a question in his eyes. It puzzled her. She felt more sure than ever that she had met him before. But that was ridiculous . . .

'Sit down, Charon . . . and you, too, Mr. Mortlake. Now you will remember your promise?' she said sternly. 'This is a delicate matter and should not be mishandled.'

'Yes, Madam,' he said politely, like a schoolboy before his headmaster, and then a smile flickered over his face: 'At least I'll try but you must admit, it's . . . it's most terribly . . .'

'Yes, I know, Mr. Mortlake. You must also

understand that it could be a great shock. Indeed, will be.' She turned to Charon, her hands folded before her, her eyes concerned, her voice kind. 'Charon, dear child, how well do you remember your parents?'

A quick flush warmed Charon's cheeks. 'Very well. I'll never—ever—forget them . . .'

'I'm sure you won't, dear. You loved them very much. They loved you, too.'

The man leaned forward. 'How old were you when they died?'

'Please . . .' Mother Superior began but Charon was not listening. She stared at the man, puzzled by the question for what business was it of his? she wondered.

'I was eight.'

'And you've been here ever since?' He sounded shocked.

She saw the flicker of pain on the Mother Superior's face and Charon spoke quickly. 'I've been very happy, here. Very happy indeed.'

'Please, Mr. Mortlake . . .'

'I'm sorry, Mother Superior,' Robin Mortlake said politely.

'Now Charon, you knew your parents loved you, didn't you?'

'Yes, Mother Superior.' Charon was getting more puzzled every moment at the strange questions. 'They were wonderful to me. I was often ill and . . . well, they were just wonderful. I loved them very much . . .'

'And they loved you?' There was a strange urgency in the Mother Superior's voice.

'I'm sure they did. I mean . . . well, it isn't something that has to be said in words, it's the way the people behave.'

'I quite agree, Charon. And they behaved well?'

'Oh, they were wonderful to me . . .' Charon looked from the Mother Superior's face to that of the man. 'I just don't understand . . .'

'Of course you don't.' The Mother Superior began to twirl the silver letter opener on her desk. Something Charon had never seen her do before.

'Charon . . . I'm not sure if I am wise in telling you this but . . . but on the other hand, I don't know that I would be wise if I didn't tell you. You have never been a very happy child . . . quiet, rather an introvert, you have retreated into a dreamland you have created for yourself. This, I fear, is because you lost your parents so suddenly and you have never overcome the shock. Now, I have to give you another shock. The Webbs were not your parents. They had adopted you.'

Charon felt as if she had been suddenly frozen to her chair. She could not move. Could hardly breathe. She had to force the words out of her dry throat.

'They adopted me?'

'Yes, Charon. They were unable to have children of their own and they adopted you.

They loved you as much, if not more, than real parents would have done.'

'I was an orphan?' Charon asked. She felt as if she was fumbling for words, rather like going through the pieces of a jigsaw puzzle, trying to make them fit, to make sense.

'No . . .'

Charon caught her breath. 'I was . . . illegitimate?'

The Mother Superior looked shocked. 'Most certainly not, dear child. Your parents came of good families.'

'But they didn't want me?' It was like a wail that tore out of her. Her mother hadn't wanted her . . .

'Charon . . .' The Mother Superior's voice was icy, like a lash on the cheek and Charon's fuddled mind cleared a little. 'I am trying to explain and you are not listening to a word I've said . . .'

Charon blinked. 'I'm sorry. I . . .'

'I know . . .' the cold voice was warmer. 'But please do me the courtesy of listening.'

Charon bowed her head. 'Of course, Mother Superior.' Charon fixed her eyes firmly on the flushed face framed by the beautiful coif the nun wore, and concentrated on what she was saying.

'Thank you. I know this is a shock, Charon dear, but you must listen to me. Your parents were very young. They were students. Your father was ill. Your mother could not cope

28

with twins as well as a sick husband. In addition, the doctor advised her to have you both adopted as you were a very delicate baby and needed extra care.'

'They didn't love me enough . . .' Charon said, the words again forcing themselves out of her terrible loneliness.

'They did love you. They wanted you . . .'

But Charon was frowning. 'You said . . . didn't you say my mother couldn't cope with *twins* . . . ?'

The man leaned forward. 'There were two of us. I'm the other one . . .'

'Mr. Mortlake . . .' The Mother Superior began but Charon was staring at Robin Mortlake. Seeing him properly for the first time. Now she began to understand why she'd thought she'd seen him before. He was a masculine Charon. They both had the same dark hair, only where hers was strictly disciplined, his was loose and allowed to grow long, curling up slightly on the nape of his neck. He was plumper than she was, too, but a healthy, sun-tanned plumpness. Her skin was pale for she was rarely in the sun. He had a quick smile, his eyes bright. She knew that her face was quiet and uninteresting, that she rarely smiled, except when she was with the children.

'Charon . . . Mr. Mortlake . . . please . . .' The Mother Superior's voice was sharp. 'I was leading up to that. A careless slip of my tongue. The truth is, Charon, I am unhappy about the situation. It is our custom to respect the parents' desires but it is not always possible to do so. When your mother brought you here as nine months old babies, she made one stipulation. That you were to be adopted together . . .'

'But we weren't . . .' Robin Mortlake began.

The elderly nun held up her hand. 'Please. I was not here at the time, Charon, but I know your mother was in tears. She said she would only give her consent to adoption if we promised you should not be separated. It was pointed out that this might prove a hazard for adoption as few people wish to adopt twins but she was adamant. She said it was bad enough for you to be separated from your mother but that you must never be separated from one another.'

'But we were . . .' Charon said. She still felt stunned with surprise. Trying to sort out her thoughts, trying to imagine her real mother. A student. How old would she have been? Nineteen, perhaps? Charon caught her breath. If she had a baby, even twins, and even a sick husband into the bargain, could she give the babies away? How could any woman—who was a real woman—do such a terrible thing? Charon had known many girls who'd had their babies adopted but there was always a real reason—even though she had never known how they could part with their babies. Into the environs of the Convent came many young unmarried mothers, girls whose parents had cast them off, refused to help them. Frightened young girls with little choice.

But her own mother had not that excuse. She was married. Couldn't she have stopped being a student and got a job? Couldn't her parents have helped them? Or his?

'Charon . . .' the Mother Superior's voice finally broke through Charon's thoughts. 'Once again, you are not listening.'

'I'm sorry, Mother Superior. I will listen . . .' Charon promised. 'It's just . . .'

'Yes, I know. Well, where was I? Oh, yes, the twins came to live with us. The boy was a fine healthy specimen, always hungry, always crying furiously because he considered he was being starved . . .' She smiled at the silent man. 'Oh, I've heard a lot about you, Mr. Mortlake.' She turned to look at Charon. 'You, my dear child, were the reverse. They found it hard to get you to eat, you had asthma, a series of colds that became bronchitis, you were never well. In fact, no one thought you would live.'

She paused, her face thoughtful. 'You were about a year old, Mr. Mortlake, when you were adopted. I was not here but I have heard many a time the story of what happened.

'The adoptive parents were a young, charming and very intelligent couple, unable to have a child. They were told that if they chose you, they must have your twin. About this time, you, Charon, became very ill indeed. The doctors thought it was hopeless. How could any adoptive parents be asked to adopt a child that has only months, perhaps weeks, in which to live? In addition, there was our side of it. We—or rather, those in charge at the time—did not deem it fair to either the Mortlakes, to the boy or to you, yourself, to allow you to be adopted. In any case, you would have needed hospitalisation. So they were allowed to adopt the boy.' She looked at Robin Mortlake. 'I take it they have been good parents? That you've been happy?'

He leant forward, hands clasped loosely between his knees. 'Extremely happy, Mother Superior.'

'And me?' Charon asked, her voice wistful.

The elderly nun turned and smiled at her.

'You, Charon, were the darling here. More prayers were said for you than had ever been said before. And a miracle happened. You survived. What is more, you became a healthy happy little girl. You were two years old when the Webbs came to look for the child they could not have. I was told that they fell in love with you at sight.'

'Because they were sorry for me?' Charon asked, her voice bitter. 'Because I was the eldest child waiting for adoption? Because I had long legs and was always in trouble?'

The Mother Superior looked shocked. 'Of course not. How were they to know that? They loved you—for you.'

Charon fidgeted. 'I thought so . . .'

'I'm certain they did. The tragedy was that they died together and so suddenly. It was a terrible shock for a small girl of eight. In addition they had no relatives to help. I wish they had told you they'd adopted you. I did speak to Mrs. Webb and she promised to tell you when you were ten years old. You would, by then, she said, know that they loved you as much, if not more, than they would have done had you been their own child.'

As Charon closed her eyes for a moment, feeling the words warm her, the Mother Superior turned to Robin Mortlake.

'You knew you were adopted?'

'Oh, yes. I grew up knowing it. Mum made a great point of it, saying how she had chosen me. She said that made me even more precious to her. She had chosen me.'

'And you knew that you had a sister?'

He shook his head violently. 'No, as I told you earlier; I had no idea until this morning.' He looked at Charon who was staring at him silently. 'If I'd known before, I'd have been here sooner,' he told her, a smile lighting up his face. 'I was thrilled to bits. I've always hated being an only child . . .'

'Why didn't she tell you before?' Charon asked stiffly.

He shrugged. 'Maybe she thought it better not for she believed you must be dead. You

33

see, it's my birthday . . .' He laughed. 'Our birthday. You're nineteen, today, too. Well, after breakfast, Mum . . . oh by the way, my father—as I'll always think of him—died two years ago and Mum has been just super. Anyhow to go back, she gave me a pair of socks at breakfast. I knew it was a joke for she is the most generous of people but I played along with her and pretended I was thrilled to death and that socks were the thing I most needed. Afterwards, she led me very casually . . .' He laughed. Such a happy sound, Charon thought.

'Oh, so very casually to the front door, opened it, and said: "Here's my real birthday present". It was a smashing car. A red M.G. sports car. Something I've always dreamed of. I guess I got a bit emotional and said I didn't deserve it and that she was the most wonderful mother in the world, and then she began to weep and that shook me rigid. You see, she doesn't cry easily and then it all came out. The sense of guilt she'd carried for years and she told me everything. All about the puny little girl baby who was going to die, and how bad she'd felt about it, but Dad had said it would be too much for her . . . and it would have ruined everything. You see . . .' His head turned from Charon to the Mother Superior as he spoke, including them both.

'You see, Mum and Dad were wild life photographers. They used to go all over the

34

world and I went along. First in a Moses Basket, later on Dad's back. It was a wonderful life and they wrote books and . . . well, did quite well and saw the world. And so did I. But Mum had never forgotten that little girl and she told me that once she came back and asked after her and heard that she'd gone. That was the phrase the nun at the gate used. A very old nun, Mum said, slightly deaf. Anyhow, Mum took it that "gone" meant she'd died, but it didn't make her feel better. She said she felt she owed it to me to tell me I'd had a sister.'

'So she told you and you . . . ?'

'Kissed her, rushed out, jumped into my new car and came here.' He smiled at them both and waved his hands. 'And have found the sister for whom I've longed all my life.'

'Mr. Mortlake . . .' the Mother Superior began and then she smiled. A warm happy smile. 'May I call you Robin?'

He beamed. 'Please do.'

She smiled and turned to Charon. 'Charon, at Robin's request, I spoke to Mrs. Mortlake on the phone. She said she would very much appreciate it if you would go and stay with them. She appears to have a false but very real feeling of guilt about you. I trust you will make her understand that this is needless. I am certain the choice was . . . or rather the decision made was out of her hands. You were, as I said, believed to be dying. It would make her very happy if you would stay with them . . .'

Charon's hand flew to her mouth. She was suddenly afraid. Two complete strangers!

'But my job . . . I mean I'm needed in the Nursery School . . .'

'You also need a holiday. We can replace you, dear child, have no fear.' She hesitated.

'As I believe I have said before, Charon, you must force yourself to face the world. I know you had a severe shock when you were eight years old. You became an introvert. You retreated into a dream world which is reality for you. You like things never to change, to be with people you know, because you feel safe that way. But you are only nineteen and you can't spend the rest of your life hiding. You understand?'

Charon nodded her head, biting her lower lip, her face frightened. 'I'll try.'

'Charon . . .' The Mother Superior sighed and turned to the silent man. 'Be gentle with her, Robin. She's led a narrow, insular and sheltered life here. She may find it hard to adjust to the world outside. Don't expect too much at first.'

She turned and stood up, going to the tall arch-shaped window and speaking over her shoulder.

'It may take many years before Charon will dare to let herself love a person. She is too afraid of being hurt to risk it. But I am grateful for your appearance and for your loving

36

reaction to the discovery that you have a sister.'

She turned to face them, her eyes worried.

'Charon, Robin has asked me the name and address of his parents. And yours, of course. I cannot give this to him. We are trusted not to reveal such knowledge and I think it would be cruel and even dangerous to do so. Your parents have grown up, have rebuilt a new life, perhaps got a family now. Memories of the past—especially of an unhappy and perhaps foolish past, can only hurt. You do understand, both of you?'

She smiled as they both nodded their heads.

'Well,' she said more cheerfully. 'Go and pack your things, Charon, and have a happy time.'

Charon drew a long shuddering breath. She looked at Robin and he smiled at her. And some of the fear in her began to dribble away. Not fast. It went slowly. Very slowly. He went on smiling and the warmth of it seemed to thaw the frozen emptiness inside her. Suddenly she realised she was no longer alone. No longer a nobody, belonging to no one, as she had thought earlier that morning.

She was someone's sister. Perhaps someone's child, if her parents still lived. Her real parents, she thought, yet somehow she couldn't think of them as her parents. The Webbs, whom she'd known so well and loved so much, they were her parents . . . Yes, but only by acceptance. By their acceptance of her, she realised. She was bound to her real parents by ties of blood, because she was part of them.

Robin waited in the cool lofty hall while she packed. Fortunately Netta was not around for she'd have bombarded Charon with questions.

Charon hadn't many things. Just the few necessary clothes. A few books. And the photograph.

She stared at it for a long time. How wonderful they'd been to her, she thought. If only she had known and could have told them.

It was quite a new experience for Charon to sit in the front seat of a racing sports car. Robin glanced at his watch.

'We'll talk over lunch. I told Mum we would. We've got to get to know one another, Charon.'

He smiled at her and a little more of the frozen emptiness inside her was chipped off.

'I'm not very good at talking,' she confessed.

He laughed as he drove away, weaving the car skilfully through the traffic. 'Oh, you'll learn. Don't worry.'

He took her to a very nice hotel where the restaurant was on a balcony which stretched out over the sea. There was a slight breeze and the sound of the waves enchanted her.

'Any particular likes or dislikes?' he asked, studying the enormous menu the waiter had given him. 'I take it you don't drink?'

She was startled. 'I never have.'

'Well, you'll have to start some time. I'll order something weak to break you in.' He grinned at her. 'Charon. I think that's a pretty name. Did you have it always?'

Again Charon was startled. 'I don't know. As long as I can remember I've been Charon.'

'It doesn't sound the sort of name the nuns would have chosen.'

'No, it doesn't. And yours?'

'Oh, Mum chose it. This Mum, I mean.' He tossed back his head and laughed. 'Gosh, isn't it confusing? I suppose we'll get used to it. Tell me, Charon, what sort of life have you had? You see, I've spent most of my life travelling and this wasn't a great help for I kept changing schools. However, Dad was good to me and I had a tutor and just studied like mad the last few years at school. Now I'm at the University studying law . . .'

Charon's eyes widened with admiration. 'You must have brains. I'm afraid I haven't. I guess it was because I've been ill a lot since . . . well, since I was born, I suppose. After my . . . my people died, I was ill for ages. I had asthma and colds and . . . I just wanted to die . . .' she finished simply.

His hand closed over hers. 'You loved them.'

'Oh, Robin, so much.' Tears filled her eyes and she blinked fast.

'You didn't do well at school?'

'I don't do well anywhere,' she said bitterly.

39

'Haven't you noticed how tall I am for a girl? I feel everyone's looking at me and having a silent giggle. I should be in a circus, one of the world's tallest girls. Look at my long legs . . . the way I walk. I'm clumsy and . . .'

'Very sorry for yourself,' he said crisply. 'We'll soon change that.' He saw her startled look and again, his hand closed tightly over hers. 'You poor little kid . . . when I think of you in that place all these years . . .'

'It wasn't so bad . . .' she said quickly. 'They were very kind to me but . . . Oh, Robin, it's a terrible feeling when you don't belong to anyone . . .' Her face was earnest and pleading. 'I know I'm being sorry for myself and I know that's wrong and that really, I'm very lucky indeed but . . . but Robin, it's so terrible when you belong to no one.'

'Well, you do, now. You belong to me.' His face clouded. 'I wish she'd told us our real names and where our parents live. I'd like to meet them. Wouldn't you?'

Charon hesitated. 'I . . . . I don't know, Robin. In a way, yes. In a way, no. I can't . . . I just can't understand how anyone can just give away her baby, let alone two babies.'

'As the Mother Superior said, she had no choice. Don't judge people, Charon, until you know all the facts. We must find our parents and learn the truth otherwise you'll have a fixation about them for the rest of your life. How can we go about it? Bust into the

40

Convent after dark and search their papers?'
He grinned at her.

Charon didn't return the smile, she was thinking. Then her face lit up. 'I know who could help us. Mrs. Jugg. She's an old darling and has been connected with the Convent since she was a baby. She'll probably know . . . She's got a cottage at Isipingo . . .'

'Good. Drink up and we'll have lunch. We'll have champagne to celebrate . . .' He smiled at her. 'And now let's start talking. What are your hobbies? I've . . .' he began.

They talked all through lunch. Oh, how they talked!

'I've never talked so much in all my life,' Charon confessed as they walked out to the parked car.

Robin's hand was warm on her arm. 'I've never enjoyed a lunch so much before. Gosh, it's good to have found you, Charon. I always wanted a kid sister . . .'

'I'm not a kid and I'm practically as tall as you . . .' Charon laughed, smiling at him.

'I'm sure I was born first . . . then that would make you my kid sister . . .' he laughed as well.

Isipingo was very hot that day. Charon had visited the old lady before so she led the way to the small cottage separated from the sea by the railway.

Mrs. Jugg was in. Startled and delighted to see them.

'Charon, my dear child, this is wonderful

'. . .' she kept saying. And when she heard their news, she wept. 'I know I'm being a silly old woman,' she said apologetically as she wiped her eyes. 'But I'm so happy for my dear Charon.'

Robin touched her hand lightly. 'She told me how wonderful you've been. You've kept her going . . .' He spoke softly for Charon had gone through to the small kitchen to make them tea. 'Mrs. Jugg, she's very bitter at times?'

'My dear boy, how can she help it? The terrible shock when her parents, as she believed them to be, died so sudden-like. She had no one at all, not even a distant cousin.'

'She had you.'

The old lady's skin was like parchment drawn taut over the bones of her face. Now she went red. 'Thank you, my dear boy, I'm grateful. It's good to know you've helped someone a little. I loved Charon like she was a grandchild. I'm happy that now she has you to care for her. I feared the day when I was gone and she would be alone . . .'

'She'll never be alone, now,' he promised. He looked through the narrow door. Charon was still out of sight and, he presumed, hearing.

'Mrs. Jugg, we've simply got to trace our parents. Charon is trying not to but she's blaming her mother for rejecting her. I don't want it to become a fixation. You know, that demoralising and soul-destroying feeling of being rejected.'

'It was not the mother's fault. Of that I'm sure,' Mrs. Jugg said slowly. 'I heard many a tale of how the young girl cried at parting from the babes. But I see what you mean. I cannot remember hearing their name but there's something . . . something I can dimly remember. Happen as we talk over tea, it'll come back to me.'

But the elusive name that Mrs. Jugg could not remember would not come and when reluctantly, Charon and Robin got ready to go, Mrs. Jugg shook her head sadly.

'I just can't remember it. Give me your phone number, Robin, my lad, and if I think on it, I'll give you a ring.'

They both kissed the frail old lady and drove away.

'I wonder if she will remember . . .' Charon said.

Robin glanced at her. 'She must. If she doesn't, we'll find another way.' He glanced at her again. 'Not scared, are you? Of meeting my Mum, I mean.'

Charon smiled weakly. 'Horribly,' she confessed. She looked down at herself. 'I didn't realise how different I looked, Robin. I think you were awfully noble to take me to that expensive restaurant with all those elegant beautiful girls about and me looking like something the cat found in the dustbin.'

He clicked his fingers before her eyes. 'Snap out of it, Charon,' he said sharply, as if angry. 'Stop being sorry for yourself and so apologetic. So maybe your hair is done old-fashioned but it's still a beautiful dark colour. Maybe your skirt is a bit long but that's your background. You couldn't wear mini-skirts in the Convent, could you. We'll change all that . . .'

'Change . . . ?' Charon sounded worried.

He laughed. 'My Mum's going to have a ball, Charon. She's always wanted a daughter and with you around, she'll go to town. Please let her enjoy herself, there's a good girl. She's very rich and has no one but me to spend her money on and now you. Let her have fun and enjoy yourself, too . . .'

'I don't understand . . .'

How Robin laughed, his dark hair ruffled by the wind as he drove fast. 'You will,' he promised.

Robin drove up to the Berea and parked the car outside a tall white house which stood alone in a big garden. He took Charon's damp hand in his and led the way up the six white steps, pressing the bell firmly.

The door opened and a big Zulu stood there, immaculately dressed in a white suit. He smiled at Robin and looked warily at Charon.

'Moses,' Robin said. 'This is my sister . . .'

'Your sister, Master?' Moses' face was puzzled. 'I didn't know as you had a sister,

44

Master.'

Robin laughed. 'Neither did I until today, Moses, that's the wonderful part. Where's the Missis?'

'Here I am, darling,' a deepish husky voice said and as Robin and Charon went in, Charon saw Mrs. Mortlake. A shortish woman, well-corseted and very elegantly dressed in a lime green shantung suit. Her bluey-white hair was elaborately groomed, her face well made-up.

Now she came forward, both hands outstretched.

'Welcome . . . welcome . . .' she said warmly.

'Mum, this is Charon . . .' Robin said, stooping to kiss the older woman. 'Charon, this is my wonderful Mum.'

Charon extended her hand and murmured politely. But Mrs. Mortlake held her hand tightly and gazed at her, almost hungrily. 'Why, you're just like Robin . . . just . . .'

'As tall and skinny but not half as handsome,' Charon said. Robin pinched her and she jumped, went bright red. 'When I first saw him, I was sure I'd seen him before but it wasn't until I learned he was my twin brother that I realised it'd been . . . well, like looking in a mirror.'

'I can see that . . .' Mrs. Mortlake gave her a quick look-over. 'I think it would suit you to have your hair short, Charon . . . and of course the Convent make you wear such ghastly long skirts. Oh . . .' She gave an absurdly skittish yet somehow endearing little jump of joy. 'What fun we're going to have.' She led the way into a tall cool room. 'I've been planning and . . .'

Robin bent and whispered in Charon's ear. 'See what I mean? She's going to have a ball. Play along with her and be kind, Charon. She really does feel badly about you.'

Charon smiled at him. 'I will,' she promised.

But it was funny, she thought, as she followed Robin and Mrs. Mortlake, that she had no feeling of rejection because the Mortlakes had refused to adopt her. Maybe it was because she had no right to expect them to want her. But with your own mother, it was different.

CHAPTER FIVE

Adam had been home just over a week when he saw his father sitting on the stoep, reading the local paper and muttering as if surprised.

It was a perfect day. Still early in the morning so that the sun was not too hot. The sky a perfect cloudless blue, the mountains tantalisingly hidden by the heat haze, the garden ablaze with flowers. The rains seemed to have left them and already the once-muddy ground was hard-baked earth.

'Well, I'll be . . .' Adam heard his father say and then give a chuckle. 'Who'da thought it . . . '

Adam was glad the old man was showing interest in something for it had been a tough week for them all. He was still having blackouts though some of the tests Gerald Fox had suggested had proved nothing. Adam had tried to make the old man feel he was still the doctor in charge, had asked his advice about the patients, discussed past histories, but the old man had been strangely permissive, doing what he was told, not even arguing when Adam suggested a complete rest. His lack of interest in everything, his complete apathy alarmed both Adam and his mother more than anything else so this sign of interest was encouraging.

'Something funny, Dad?' Adam asked, relaxing in a wicker chair by his father's side.

The old man looked up and passed him the paper.

'Take a look at that photo, son, and tell me who it reminds you of . . .'

Adam frowned slightly as he gazed at the picture of a man and girl. Or perhaps, he thought, it should be a boy and girl. They looked as if they were in their late teens. Both extraordinarily alike. Identical twins, perhaps? Both had very thick dark hair, cut short, very dark eyes, high cheekbones, full generous mouths. The girl looked a bit scared but the boy was completely at ease, glancing at her with very obvious affection.

47

'They do remind me of someone . . .' Adam said slowly, racking his brain. He stared at the girl. There was a vague familiarity in the face and yet it was completely different from what he vaguely remembered. Her hair was cut very short, what was, he believed, today called the 'Twiggy-cut', but the look of fear, of wariness in her eyes still reminded him of someone.

'Of course they do . . .' his father said triumphantly. 'Eleanor Lillington!'

'Eleanor . . .' Adam echoed slowly, frowning a little, trying to connect the name with a face.

'Oh, Adam . . . of course you know her,' Henry Bray said impatiently. 'She came up to see your mother the first night you were here.'

'Oh, yes, I remember . . .'

Adam sat back and relaxed as Sarah, the housegirl, brought out a tray of coffee. He passed the sugar basin to his father and then helped himself.

'A tall woman, jet black hair. Dark eyes. A rather deep pleasant voice. Bursting with energy. Made me wonder what she was doing here. I felt she'd be happier sitting in Parliament or wearing a barrister's wig . . .'

The older man exploded with laughter. 'Not bad, Adam, not bad, at all. Only one thing wrong. She's content. Not missing the conflict of public life, I'd say. She is a happy woman, has four delightful children, a kind and good husband, a flourishing farm. In addition she sits on every committee there is and visits all the elderly lonely people in the district. She's a do-gooder but in the right way. Like your mum, Eleanor loves people. That's why she and Eleanor get on so well. A fine woman . . .'

'Then what's so funny about the photo?'

The older man leaned forward and with a long finger pointed to some small printing. 'Just read that, son.'

Frowning, Adam read the small print.

'Urgently need information regarding birth of twins nineteen years ago in Durban. Knowledge of parents small except that they came from AMANZI. Please help.'

'Rather an odd advert . . .' Adam said slowly.

His father nodded. 'Could throw a spanner in someone's works. I reckon they must be Eleanor's kids. She was married before but her husband died. Sam Lillington is her second husband.'

'But she's not old enough to have children of nineteen.'

'She's thirty-seven. She got married at seventeen.'

'But she's not . . .'

'The type of woman to desert her kids?' Henry Bray asked, putting down his cup. 'I agree. Probably a reason. From what I gather, she married a weakling. They were students. We weren't here in those days but I've heard tell she was a wild girl. A real rebel. Tell her she couldn't or mustn't do a thing, and she

49

promptly did it. Anyhow, I wonder how Sam'll feel, suddenly having twin stepchildren.' He chuckled. 'Knowing Sam, I guess he'll be delighted. Got a great big heart, that Sam, and mad about kids. Lucky Eleanor married such a decent chap, I reckon.'

'But this is pure hypothesis, Dad. Just because there is a vague likeness . . .'

'Vague, is it, my boy? I bet there are tongues wagging in town today . . .'

How right he was, Adam discovered as he went about his daily duties. In the hospital, the Matron, a big formidably unfriendly woman, seemed to have thawed.

'Seen the paper, Doctor? Oh, I forgot, you're practically a stranger here.'

The nurses as he went from ward to ward seemed to have a hushed excitement, glancing quickly at one another, giving a little giggle and then looking very innocent.

As Adam went from bed to bed, glancing at the charts, asking questions, he thought how surprising it was that in this blossoming small African state, there was still so much belief in witchcraft, as evidenced by the large number of babies, children and adults who'd been treated by witchdoctors and then brought in here for the white doctors to repair the damage.

He drove down into the small town to the room he used as a surgery for an hour each morning. As he parked his car, he saw the woman everyone appeared to be talking about—Eleanor Lillington—hurrying towards him.

A tall, slender well-dressed woman with jet black hair and dark eyes, she was smiling excitedly.

'Oh, Adam, have you seen the paper? Isn't it wonderful?'

'Isn't what wonderful?' he asked, noting how well-cut was the blue linen suit, what an air of efficiency she gave.

'Why, the twins, Adam. Didn't you see them in the paper? They're my twins . . .' Her cheeks were flushed, her voice excited. 'It's the most wonderful thing in the world, Adam. I had no choice. Tim, that was my husband, was ill and . . . well, he was ill and there was absolutely no money at all. We were both students and . . . well, everything was just too grim for words. Then the baby girl was terribly ill all the time, and I had to work and . . . well . . .' She shrugged her shoulders. 'The doctor said it would be kinder to the children in the long run and . . .'

Adam, looking at her, saw her eyes suddenly fill with tears.

'It must have been tough,' he said quietly.

'Oh, it was. Sheer hell, Adam. Then . . . then Tim died and . . . well, you know how it is when you give up your kids for adoption. They'll never tell you anything at all. After I'd married Sam, I went back to see if they were

51

all right. They'd been adopted and I was assured that both were very happy and much loved so . . .' She sighed. 'Well, I just tried to forget them. Then we had our four kids and now this . . . this just coming out of the blue . . .'

Adam was vaguely aware of passers-by glancing at them curiously, of the heat of the sun as it rose higher in the sky, but his attention was gripped by the woman to whom he was talking.

'It must have been a shock . . .'

'Oh, it was.' Her face was radiant. 'A wonderful shock. We don't have the papers delivered—we live too far out and so I only knew just now when I went into Cox's to collect the newspapers. I couldn't believe my eyes. They're the spitting image of me . . .'

Adam smiled. 'That's what Dad said.'

'That's what everyone's saying.' Eleanor Lillington laughed happily, then her face clouded. 'Now I'm rushing home to tell Sam before some kind, well-meaning friend steps in . . .'

'He doesn't know?'

She shook her head. 'No. Of course, he knew I'd been married but . . . well, quite honestly, Adam, I was scared stiff. You see, Sam's crazy about kids. We talked about them for hours. He was always saying he could never understand how any woman—who was a real woman—could part with her children. I was afraid if I told him about the twins, that he'd think I'd been callous and . . . well, and cold and . . .' She paused, her face worried. 'Oh, I do hope I can make him understand . . .'

'I'm sure you will . . . It's just . . .'

She looked at him enquiringly. 'How would you react, Adam? I mean if you were in Sam's shoes?'

He hesitated. 'That's a tough question. I mean, I've never been married or a father.'

'You must have some feeling about it? Would you be angry with me for not telling you? Would you think I was a monster . . .?'

Adam put his hand on her arm. 'I wouldn't be angry,' he said quickly. 'I might be hurt. I might wonder where I'd failed . . .'

'Where you'd failed?' She looked puzzled. 'Aren't you reversing things? I'm the one who's failed . . .'

'I don't see it that way. I'd feel that somehow I'd failed you because you couldn't trust me enough to believe I'd understand. After all, when you love a person, you should be able to tell them anything and know that they'd understand, shouldn't you? If you can't trust them like that, then you can't . . .' He paused, gave an uneasy laugh. 'I'm getting rather involved . . .'

Eleanor looked at him curiously. 'Have you ever been in love?'

He shook his head. 'Not really. Infatuated, perhaps.'

'You set high standards, Adam. I wonder if you'll ever meet anyone who comes up to them.'

'If I don't, I shan't get married.' He smiled. 'It's as simple as that.'

'You make it sound so easy . . .' She laughed. 'Well, give your Mum and Dad my love and tell them I'll pop up later. Now I must rush and tell Sam—and then tell the kids. I wonder how they'll react . . .'

'The twins look a nice couple.'

'He does . . .! You know, Adam, I looked like he does when I was young. That happy, sure of yourself, optimistic, friendly look. The girl rather worries me. She looks scared stiff. I wonder what's happened to her . . .' Again, Adam heard the note of anxiety in Eleanor Lillington's voice. 'Know something, Adam? Being a parent is tough. No matter what you do, no matter how hard you try to do the right thing, you're landed with an outsize sense of guilt.'

'I don't think you need feel that way about the twins,' he said quickly. 'In the doctor's place, I'm sure I'd have given you the same advice.'

'I only wish I knew if I did do the right thing . . .' Eleanor said with a deep sigh. Then smiled. 'Thanks for lending me your shoulder to lean on, Adam. One day, some lucky girl's going to walk down the aisle with you. See you later.'

She waved her hand and hurried to her parked car. He stood still, staring after her. He wondered how she'd tell her husband, how he'd react, what the four children would think, and—above all—what she planned to do. He felt almost positive that the first thing she'd do when she'd told her husband, was to sit down and write a long letter to the twins. Nineteen years was a long time. A very long time to be without a mother.

CHAPTER SIX

Charon was in her bedroom with 'Aunt Irene' when the letter came. With her hair cut short, 'Twiggy-way', Charon looked a very different person from the quiet girl who had sat, holding the hysterical child tightly, in the Children's Ward at St. Christopher's Hospital.

Now as she kept trying to attach the false eyelashes, she suddenly laughed and the elegantly-dressed older woman looked pleased.

'You really are enjoying this, Charon?' Irene Mortlake asked.

Charon turned her head to smile. 'Honestly, Aunt Irene, you can't imagine how much fun this is. I just don't know how to start thanking you for all those lovely clothes . . .'

'Then don't try, please. Just by seeing you

look so much happier, is all the reward I want. Why, already you're a different girl . . .'

'I feel different, too. Completely different.' For a moment Charon's face was relaxed and she looked absurdly young and, Irene Mortlake thought, pathetically vulnerable.

But Charon had not said all she thought for she knew it hurt 'Aunt Irene' to be reminded of Charon's years at the Orphanage. What was really in Charon's mind was that the chief reason for feeling so 'different' was this wonderful knowledge that she 'belonged' to someone. Even if Robin had not been such a wonderful person, he would still have been her twin brother, which made it impossible for her to be alone and on her own.

It was then that Robin burst into the room, waving an opened envelope.

'She's written . . . she's written . . .' he shouted excitedly.

Charon turned round and stared at him. Vaguely she noticed the luxurious furniture, the slim bed with its blue silk cover, the matching curtains, the vase of roses, the huge wardrobe full of the new clothes 'Aunt Irene' had bought her but inside her she felt very cold.

'She . . . ?' Charon said very quietly.

'Yes, our mother. She wants us to go up—at once and stay with them.'

Charon ran her tongue nervously over her dry lips.

56

'Them?' She could feel the cold chill sliding down her backbone.

Robin laughed. 'And how! She has four kids. The eldest is fourteen and the youngest four. This is her second marriage. It seems her first husband, our father, is dead . . . He died . . .'

'Before we . . . we were adopted?' Charon almost whispered. That would be a legitimate reason for having your babies adopted—a girl on her own . . .

'No, after, I gather. She says he was very ill and she had no choice but to . . .'

Charon was not listening. She had turned back to the mirror, leaning forward, and now patiently tried to adjust the false eyelashes that kept sliding down her cheek.

'We'll drive up, Charon . . .' The odd note in Robin's voice made Irene Mortlake turn to look at this young man who was suddenly a stranger.

'I don't want to see her,' Charon said very quietly.

'You've no choice, my child,' Robin said gaily but there was a hint of steel in his voice, Irene Mortlake noted. 'This is our bounden duty. In any case, don't forget we've got to find out which of us is the senior. It's pretty important to me. I always did want a kid sister . . .' He winked at Irene Mortlake as she stood there, puzzled and a little bewildered.

'By the way, Mum,' Robin went on. 'You don't mind if Charon and I nip up to meet our new relations, do you?'

Somehow Irene Mortlake forced a smile to her suddenly stiff face. This was the fear most adoptive parents have—that one day the real parents will turn up and claim the children that have been yours for years.

'Of course not, darling,' she made herself say brightly. 'We must start planning clothes and things. When are you off?'

'The sooner the better,' Robin declared, watching Charon as she leaned forward to stare at her reflection in the mirror. 'I'll send her a wire to say when to expect us.'

After 'Aunt Irene' and Robin had left her, Charon sat for a long time, her flushed face in her hands, her eyes staring blindly at the reflection in the mirror that looked so very different from the Charon she had known for years. There was no doubt but that 'Aunt Irene' had made the most of Charon's shortcomings. The short hair added strength and character to the pale face. The make-up, skilfully applied, added beauty. The clothes, wisely chosen, made her long slender body almost beautiful, making the most of what Aunt Irene called: 'your gorgeous model-legs'. Already some of Charon's self-confidence had been restored, she no longer felt self-conscious when Robin took her out, or ashamed for him in case people wondered who the ghastly female he was with could be! The gay young clothes were fun, too. This was an entirely new aspect of living to Charon but now, quite suddenly, the happiness had been wiped out.

She didn't want to go to Amanzi. To see her mother who had successfully forgotten her twin babies for nineteen years!

She didn't really hate her mother, Charon told the girl in the mirror, who looked at her with wide unhappy eyes. Not really hate her. It was more of a feeling of . . . well, of not wanting to make her mother remember her if she didn't want to . . . Oh, it was all so involved.

Robin was worried. He'd made that plain. He thought she had a fixation or something about her mother.

'You can't go through the rest of your life hating someone for something that may not have been her fault,' he'd said sternly.

He seemed to find it unnatural and strange that she didn't want to rush to Amanzi, throw her arms round her unknown mother and immediately love her.

You couldn't turn on love—as though it was a tap of water. There when needed, but discreetly out of sight when a nuisance.

Love grew because of things that happened. Already Charon knew she was finding she loved Robin for his laughter and affection; that she was beginning to love Aunt Irene because she was so good to her, and not at all possessive where Robin was concerned though it was obvious that she just adored Robin. And who could blame her?

Just because a woman had a baby, surely it didn't mean that automatically the baby loved her?

Yet . . .

Her thoughts skidded to a standstill. Yet wasn't that what she demanded of her mother, Charon asked herself.

She had been taught to be honest, to look at problems objectively. Now if she denied the necessity of automatically loving her mother . . . then what right had she to expect her mother to automatically love her?

Charon stood up and began to walk round the room, her feet sinking into the deep pile of the cream carpet.

If only her father had lived, she thought unhappily. She'd always longed for a father. The man she had believed to be her father had been so wonderful, calling her his 'lovely lass', playing with her, telling her a good-night story and tucking her up with a bedtime hug. Although she had loved her 'mother' very much, Charon realised suddenly that it was her 'father' she had missed most.

Now she had a new real mother and a new step-father and some step-sisters and brothers. How would they feel about the strangers suddenly walking in? Wouldn't they resent them?

How she dreaded the thought of meeting them all. So many strangers and no face there she knew.

And then she felt ashamed. Robin would be there. Robin who'd been so good to her, who meant so much to her already. She mustn't spoil his excitement at meeting his real mother, she musn't spoil anything for him.

The journey up to Amanzi was delightful. Driving through the Valley of a Thousand Hills, then past the great Drakensberg mountains and through miles and miles of mountainous, almost uninhabited country, some of Charon's fear vanished and she relaxed in the M.G. sports car by Robin's side. They were always talking yet they never seemed to run out of something to talk about.

Sometimes Charon was afraid she might bore Robin for her life had been insular and often drab, whereas his was like a fairy tale of different exotic countries, strange people and exciting events.

They had left Durban soon after four a.m. and it was late afternoon when they crossed the border into Amanzi and followed the signposts' directions to Ukoma.

Charon felt absurdly disappointed when they reached it. She didn't know what she had expected but hardly this one street of stores and garages and the great mountains all round standing sentinel on the lush valley. The sun was hot, even the breeze warm but up here in the mountains the air felt different.

Robin stopped the car outside a store and

looked at the letter he must have read a hundred times.

'Through the town, over the bridge, first turning on left where it says to the Airport, then third gate on right. You can't mistake the citrus trees. You'll see them miles away,' Robin read out aloud and passed Charon the letter. 'Now check as I go, Charon. I'm the world's worst navigator.'

'Then I must be the second worst . . .' she laughed, trying to stifle the fear that was growing inside her.

Soon they would be there. How did you greet a mother you've never known, she wondered. Suppose they hated one another at sight? Or suppose one of them liked the other, and the other disliked the first? And what sort of husband had she? And the kids? Charon usually got on well with kids but maybe these would be different . . .

Robin drove through the town and the brief spell of macadamised road became the dusty earth road again, then down a steep hill, sharp left over a frighteningly narrow bridge with low railings over a river that was spuming whitely, the water swirling over stones and falling in tiny cascades towards a biggish pool.

'Looks like they've had quite a bit of rain already,' Robin said, driving over it. 'Now first turning right . . . ?'

Charon was trying to read the words. 'No, Robin, first left. It says . . . says something about an Airport . . .'

'Here we are . . .' He slowed up and on the signpost was a notice AIRPORT TWO MILES AHEAD.

'We could have flown up. I didn't realise there was an airport . . .' Robin said.

'I think this was much nicer,' Charon told him.

He grinned. 'So do I. I've enjoyed it. Now keep me in line, Charon. What do we do next?'

'Third gate on right. She said something about citrus . . .'

'That's it . . .' Robin shouted triumphantly. About a mile further on, the road began to climb and they could see the citrus trees marching in neat lines up the mountainside. They turned in the white gate that was waiting open for them, along a winding drive between tall trees that overhung and embraced one another above their heads, and then they saw the house.

A big double-storied white house with a wide stoep all round it. There was a car parked in front outside it. A rather old-looking red car.

And then they were there and a group of people came hurrying outside and a roar of voices swept towards them. Somehow Charon got out. She saw a tall dark-haired woman greeting Robin and she stared blankly at the group of children with a short stoutish man with a sun-tanned face and sandy hair and another man . . .

Charon caught her breath with relief. They were not all strangers. This man she knew . . .

She half stumbled towards him. 'Dr. Bray . . .' she said breathlessly. 'Oh, Dr. Bray . . . I want to thank you for helping Christine . . .'

The tall man came towards her, his face puzzled.

'You're the . . .'

'I was at St. Christopher's Hospital when you came to see Christine. Don't you remember?' she asked anxiously. Suddenly it had become overwhelmingly important that he *did* remember, that he did know her.

His face changed. He smiled and his stern look vanished.

'Why—you're the girl with the braided hair . . . No wonder I didn't quite recognise your photo in the paper.'

He had taken her hand and was holding it in a warm, tight grasp and she gazed at him with relief.

'Yes. I know I look different. Very different . . .' she spoke fast, as if afraid to stop talking because of what might lie ahead. 'Oh, Dr. Bray, I was so grateful and so was Christine. I went in to see her just before we left and she's fine.'

The Doctor smiled. 'They operated on her?'

'Yes, and they say everything's fine and I'm sure it's thanks to you. She was so afraid of leaving St. Christopher's.'

He let go her hand and smiled. 'I'm so glad. I merely spoke to Dr. Fox. He arranged everything . . .'

'But if you hadn't spoken to him . . .' Charon said earnestly. And then Robin was there.

'Charon . . .' he said. 'I want you to meet . . .'

Reluctantly Charon turned and found herself staring into the face of an equally tall woman with equally dark hair and equally dark eyes. A woman who looked just like Robin but for one thing. Her eyes. And as she stared at her mother, Charon realised that her mother had *her* eyes—the eyes of a frightened woman.

Charon didn't know what she had expected her mother to look like. But the last thing in the world she had expected was to see such open fear.

CHAPTER SEVEN

Adam found himself staring at Charon, for he could not reconcile this girl with the quiet permissive girl in the Hospital. Now he noticed the strangely dismayed look on her face as Eleanor Lillington greeted her. Was it dismay, Adam wondered, or shock? If so, why had she looked shocked? He could see, as well as sense, that Charon had not come to meet her real mother willingly and this also surprised

65

him, for as a rule adopted children are eager to meet their real parents.

Now as Charon stood there, a stiff smile fixed to her face, Sam Lillington, whom Adam hardly knew, moved forward.

'Welcome, Charon,' he said. A short man, too plump to please a doctor, his tanned cheeks slightly red, but his voice was kind. 'We're delighted to meet you. These are the kids . . .' He waved his hand towards the four children. 'Pippa . . . as you can guess from her jodhpurs, is a horse lover. . .'

Pippa, a tall girl with red hair, surprisingly mature, Adam thought, for her fourteen years, grinned but her eyes left Charon instantly and were drawn, as if fascinated, to the tall handsome new step-brother.

'Jeremy . . .' Sam introduced with a wave of his hand. 'Crazy about sports and pop tunes but not so keen on school . . .' He grinned at the tall twelve-year-old, whose hair was dark like his mother's and whose body was lean and strong.

'Hi . . .' he said, waving a hand in greeting politely but he, too, Adam noticed, turned to look again at Robin, as if sizing him up.

'Keith . . .' Sam went on and his voice changed, became—Adam thought—softer, more gentle.

The short red-headed boy, standing behind the older children, gave a shy smile. Keith was the child that Adam knew most about. He had frequent bursts of asthma. Adam's father had discussed the case with Adam and said it was his opinion they were purely of nervous origin because Keith suffered from an outsize inferiority complex with his older brother and sister, both brilliant at sport and quite bright at school.

'And of course, the monster . . .' Sam said, his voice proud as he bent and lifted the four-year-old Midge on to his back. 'I warn you, Charon, she may look like a little angel but . . .' He turned to smile at the girl clinging to his neck, 'What say? Sweetheart?'

'I'm a good girl, Daddy . . .' she said, her mouth pouting for a moment and then relaxing into the sweetest, most beguiling smile imaginable. 'I'm Daddy's best girl . . .' she added.

Midge was also dark, like her mother, her hair cut short and curling round her face. The youngest and the most spoilt, Adam thought, but who could blame them, he wondered. One day, Midge was going to break a great many masculine hearts.

'Do come inside . . .' Eleanor said eagerly, her voice a little uneven, Adam noticed.

'I should go . . .' he began but Sam turned to him at once.

'Of course not, Adam . . .'

And Eleanor said: 'They know where you are, don't they?'

But perhaps what made Adam decide to

stay, although he felt this was purely a family affair and he was odd man out, was the quick imploring look Charon gave him. An urgent despairing look. It reminded him of the way she'd looked in the Children's Ward as she begged him to make them let Christina stay in the hospital and not be transferred.

Adam sat with Sam on the wide patio that overlooked the heart-shaped swimming pool, while the children seemed to vanish and Eleanor showed Robin and Charon their bedrooms.

Sam filled his pipe slowly and then glanced at Adam.

'So what?' he asked.

Adam frowned. 'So what—what?' he parried.

Sam jerked his head towards the house behind. 'How'll it work out and why is the girl so scared?'

'I think she's always a bit scared—it's not only this . . . well, this rather unusual situation.'

Sam's face lost its worried look. 'I thought she'd be thrilled to bits to find her real mother,' he admitted.

'Most girls are but we don't know all the background, do we?'

'That's true . . .'

When Eleanor joined them, with Robin close behind, and Charon far in the rear, Sam got them all drinks. He looked at the twins thoughtfully.

'We'd be grateful if you'd put us in the picture, both of you. Your mother's worried about you both a great deal but she knew you'd been adopted and that you were happy.'

Adam glancing at Charon saw the way her lips curled bitterly. Her hands were folded in her lap, her eyes downcast. A typical Convent product, he thought, and knew fresh sympathy with her. His sympathy grew when she told them of her life, her voice quiet and unemotional, except when she described the day she'd come home from school and found the house empty.

'The Webbs had no relations at all so I was sent to the orphanage. I was too old then for anyone to want to adopt me so I just stayed there.'

Eleanor leaned forward. 'Were they good to you?'

Charon lifted her head and looked at her. A strange blank look, Adam noticed.

'Who? The Webbs or the Convent? The Webbs were wonderful people. I . . . I loved them very much. That's what made it so awful when . . . when they died. Of course I thought they were my real parents. They were going to tell me they'd adopted me but . . . but they said they'd tell me when I was ten years old, Mother Superior said.'

'You didn't know . . . know you'd been adopted by them?' Eleanor said gently.

Charon shook her head. She looked pale

and tired.

'Not until Robin came along . . .'

Eleanor turned to Robin. 'And you . . . ?'

He stretched out his long legs. He was wearing khaki shorts and a thin white shirt. He'd obviously had a quick shower for his dark hair was wet. He looked completely at ease. In fact, Adam thought, he looked the happiest of them all.

'I always knew I was adopted. Mum saw to that. She said it can be a terrible shock . . .' He looked at Charon. 'I'm afraid the poor kid had a lot of shocks that day.' He smiled at her. 'Didn't you?'

Charon smiled. It was the first time Adam had seen her smile. How it changed her, he thought at once. How young it made her look—how young and helpless.

'I certainly had but . . .' She flushed slightly. 'All the same, Robin, it was an absolutely heavenly day. I enjoyed every moment of it . . .'

'Meeting Robin, you mean?' Eleanor asked. She, too—Adam thought—looked tired and strained.

Charon nodded. 'It was so utterly wonderful to discover that I belonged to someone. You see, before, I had no one. No one at . . .' Her hand flew to her mouth and her eyes, dismayed, looked at Eleanor, then round at each face in turn. She reminded Adam of a rabbit, chased and cornered. 'I mean . . .' Charon went on hastily. 'The nuns were marvellous. I couldn't have been happier but . . . but now I'm grown-up and earning my living, well . . . one felt sort of lonely at times and . . .'

'I'm sure you did,' Sam said comfortably, getting up to fill their glasses. 'I'm an orphan so I know how you felt. Go on, Robin, what made you suddenly search out your sister?'

Robin jumped up to help him, telling them of his birthday present, of his Mum's feeling of guilt about the twin they didn't adopt . . .

Eleanor leaned forward angrily. 'But I made them promise to have you both adopted together.'

It was Charon, this time, who came to the rescue.

'Oh, we know. Mother Superior told us that you'd insisted on it but you see, it wasn't anyone's fault. When Aunt Irene—that's what I call Mrs. Mortlake—adopted Robin, I was dying. At least that's what the doctors said. I had only a few weeks to live, they said and they won't allow children to be adopted like that . . . She's very upset about it but it really wasn't her fault . . .'

Adam saw Eleanor close her eyes for a minute as Robin went on.

'What makes it all worse is that Mum always longed for a daughter but they only had me. She did go back to the orphanage and heard that Charon had gone . . . she thought it meant that she had died.'

71

'I went back, too . . .' Eleanor said bluntly. 'They told me you were both adopted and very happy.'

'We were . . .' Charon said at once, 'then. It wasn't anyone's fault that the Webbs died . . .' Her eyes suddenly filled with tears but she turned her head away and sipped her drink.

Robin jumped into the conversation. 'Do tell us, which of us was born first?' he said eagerly.

Eleanor smiled. 'You were—two hours before . . . Charon.'

Robin got up and did a little dance, then leant across to Charon and pulled her hair gently.

'So . . .' he said triumphantly. 'You are my kid sister, Charon, you are my kid sister! Watch your step now or Big Brother will discipline you . . .'

She looked at him and they both laughed. What a strong bond of love had grown up between them already, Adam thought.

'Another thing,' Robin said eagerly. 'What were our real names? I mean, I know Mum chose Robin for me and I imagine the Webbs chose Charon. What did you call us?'

A strange and obviously uncomfortable flush reddened Eleanor Lillington's face.

'We didn't really name you . . .' She began to pleat the soft batiste material of her yellow dress. 'You see, Tim . . . that was your father, and I couldn't agree about names. So for the

72

time being I called you Boy and . . . and Girlie. It sounds rather daft, I know, but . . .'

'I was very delicate, wasn't I?' Charon asked.

Eleanor looked at her. 'Very. It was frightening. I knew so little, nothing about babies and . . . well, it was terrible.'

'Mother Superior said I was one of their miracles,' Charon told them. 'No one thought I would live . . .'

'Just shows how wrong doctors can be . . .' Robin grinned at Adam. 'Present company always excepted. I bet you'll live to be ninety, Charon, my chicken.'

'Ninety . . .' Charon said slowly. 'Another seventy-one years . . .'

She spoke dubiously as though the idea didn't appeal to her. Sitting silently, Adam found himself watching her every movement, the turn of her head, the wariness of her eyes, the caution with which she spoke, the dismay she showed if she felt she'd said the wrong thing or had spoken out of turn. A great wave of sympathy enveloped him. What sort of life had she led those last eleven years? Disciplined, taught to respect and obey her elders, to look demure, to speak when spoken to, to accept what she was told without discussion, to walk alone . . . so terribly alone. Perhaps it was worse because of her memories. She'd obviously loved the Webbs very much and they had idolised her. How terrible it must be when you are eight and suddenly become a 'no one', just another number in a group of parentless girls. You are suddenly cut off from loving and being loved. You no longer have your own bedroom, your cherished toys, your parents to fuss over you and spoil you.

There must have been a terrible finality about it—like the clean sharp cut of a guillotine's knife. No wonder the child had retreated into herself, was wary, nervous of what might happen.

And the double shock. The first of learning that her parents had not been her parents, that they had adopted her and that she belonged to no one. Then the shock of learning that her parents, her real parents, had—as it would seem to her—rejected her . . . No wonder the girl looked tired and bewildered. What an upheaval . . . !

An African house-boy came out and spoke to Sam, he looked at Adam.

'Duty calls, old man, I'm afraid . . .' he said with a smile. 'The hospital wants you. Sounds pretty urgent . . .'

Adam jumped up. 'Thanks. I'm on my way . . .'

Eleanor got up. 'I'll see you out . . .'

At that moment, the children came running round the side of the house. 'Come for a swim, Robin?' Pippa shouted.

Robin waved. 'Not today, Pippa, thanks. Charon and I have had a pretty hectic day. We feel like flopping just now . . .'

Pippa, in a white bikini which showed off her suntanned, well-developed body to advantage, gave a little grimace.

'Cissy . . .' she shouted and did a perfect dive into the pool.

Jeremy jumped in after her, diving deep, coming up to duck her so that she squealed and clawed at his hair, laughing as she shook herself.

Keith went down the steps slowly, glancing up at the 'oldies'. Adam looked at Charon and saw the dismay written plainly on her face for all to see. He wondered if she could swim. He found himself sincerely hoping so!

Eleanor walked silently by his side to the old red car. As he got into it, she looked down at him.

'She didn't seem too pleased to see me,' she said slowly.

Adam looked up at her. 'Don't push her,' he told her. 'She's still suffering from the shock. Give her time and I'm sure she will be quite different.'

Eleanor's drawn face brightened. 'You think so?'

'I do. Just give her time. She needs it, Eleanor.'

'But Robin's so different. Already I feel we're close to one another. They are twins and I'd have thought . . .'

'But they were brought up in totally

75

different environments. Don't forget that she had no idea, until quite recently, that the Webbs were not her real parents. That was a bad enough shock and . . .'

'Added to which shock, she obviously is convinced I never wanted them—the twins, I mean. You can feel it in the atmosphere,' Eleanor said unhappily.

'I know,' Adam started the engine and slid into gear. 'Just give her time, as I said. Try to see it through her eyes. She's not used to strangers, you know. Nor this sort of life. Be affectionate but don't make too much fuss of her. What I'm trying to say is, don't make an issue of it. Just accept her and take it for granted she'll accept you, but don't expect an emotional reaction. She's been disciplined to hide and control her emotions. It won't be easy for her to unwind . . .'

'Thanks very much, Adam,' Eleanor said and stood back. 'You've helped me a lot.'

She watched the car go and then walked, very slowly, back into the house.

CHAPTER EIGHT

There was plenty of work waiting at the hospital for Adam. There'd been a fight in the township and several Africans brought in with stab wounds as well as a child who'd been running across the road by the bus terminus and been knocked down. An emergency operation had to be performed and just as Adam thought he could go home, Dr. Hlamanu, one of the doctors, asked Adam's advice about a baby who was not responding to treatment.

By the time Adam had parked the old red car outside his home, he realised how hungry he was! His mother was out but his father was waiting for him.

'Your dinner's in the oven, son,' he said, lowering his newspaper and peering over his glasses. 'Had a day, I gather? I heard there'd been a bit of a fight. What about a drink?'

Adam had flung himself down into the deep, leather-covered armchair. 'Bright of you, Dad, just what I need. I'll get it.'

'Indeed you won't,' his father said at once, pulling himself up out of his chair. 'I'm not quite helpless.'

He poured out two stiff drinks, gave Adam one and went back to his chair.

'Well, and what are Eleanor's twins like?' he asked. Adam gulped down his drink and went and refilled the glass.

'Exactly like Eleanor,' he said. 'Where's Ma . . . ?'

Henry sighed. 'Out at one of her meetings. She's talking about something or other. The twins . . . have they got their mother's brains?' he asked eagerly.

Adam grinned. 'Give us a chance, Dad, why I've hardly said two words to 'em. Rather interesting, though, they are completely different in their reaction to all of this. Now Charon . . . oddly enough, I'd seen her before . . .'

He leaned forward, grateful that the old man was showing so much interest in something, also glad of the chance to put his thoughts into words, repeating what the twins had said.

'My personal opinion,' Adam finished, 'is that the girl is still in a state of shock. It's all happened so fast that she's unable to adjust herself.'

His father nodded slowly. 'I think you're right, son. Pretty overwhelming. How d'you think it'll work out?'

'Given time and understanding, it should be all right. I should imagine she's a decent kid. Got ideals and compassion, all right. She wouldn't hurt anyone if she could help it. My only fear is that Eleanor will get emotional about it. You can't turn love on and off, like switching on an electric light . . . It's got to grow.'

The older man chuckled. 'You're so right, son. What about you, eh? Your mother was talking about Marie Fox? Anything coming of that?'

'Marie?' Adam realised suddenly that he had completely forgotten Marie! He chuckled

78

silently, thinking how furious she would be could she read his thoughts. 'Oh, Marie's all right if you're the right kind of man. Afraid I'm not. She wants the social type. A successful, extremely wealthy man who'll do everything she demands. I don't come under any of those headings.'

'Thank God you don't, son. Now what about something to eat?' He pressed the bell by his side and the houseboy came hurrying, going back to the kitchen and returning with a tray and Adam's favourite meal: cauliflower au gratin.

'I was hungry, Dad,' Adam said when he'd cleared the plate, and eaten the peaches and cream that followed. He yawned. 'As you said, it's been quite a day.'

'I reckon you won't need rocking tonight, Adam,' his father chuckled as they both made their way to their rooms. 'Looks like your mum's got caught up,' Henry chuckled. 'She does enjoy these meetings, you know. I just can't understand it. Give me my chair, my cigarette and my newspaper and I'm happy.'

'Plus your brandy,' Adam teased.

His father's face changed. 'You reckon I should give up drinking, Adam?'

Adam hesitated, saw the anxiety in his father's eyes.

'As your doctor, I might feel compelled to say yes,' Adam told him. 'As your son, I'd say, to hell no. The amount you drink couldn't harm a fly.'

Henry Bray laughed, and put his hand on Adam's shoulder.

'You're a good son, Adam, though I say it myself. I couldn't have put it better if I'd tried.'

In bed, Adam stretched his weary limbs but somehow sleep eluded him. He found himself thinking of that girl. Charon. An odd name. Yet strangely attractive. An odd girl, too. He wondered if she was also finding it hard to sleep. If she was lying on her back, gazing at the ceiling, remembering . . .

Remembering the Webbs, whom she'd loved so much. Remembering those terrible months after their deaths and the slow acceptance of not belonging to anyone, of walking alone. How terrible it must be to have to accept it, he thought. Plumping up his pillow, turning it in a vain effort to find a cool spot for his hot cheek, Adam sighed. It wasn't going to be easy for either Charon or for her mother, he thought.

A week later, he met Charon in town. It had been a hard tough week for Adam, unused to the life of a G.P. as he was; of late night calls that often proved unnecessary, of long drawn-out stretches by the bedsides of patients who seemed determined to die and whom he was equally determined to save. What amazed him was how often they still came across cases of Africans who had been put under a 'spell' and who just turned their faces to the wall and accepted the fact that they must die. This was something no drugs could fight. It left him with a furious yet futile sense of helplessness. He and Dr. Dhlamini held long arguments about it. Wasn't it high time that educated Africans shed this age-old fear, Adam would demand. And Roger Dhlamini would shake his dark handsome head and smile tolerantly.

'It is something engraved in our bodies,' he said with a shrug. 'Even your people have their superstitions,' he pointed out with a smile. 'How many will walk under a ladder or get married on the 13th? Is it not the truth that many hotels do not have rooms numbered thirteen?' he asked with a chuckle.

'That's different . . .' Adam would begin and they would both end up by laughing and agreeing that it was a funny world.

'Only . . .' Dr. Dhlamini held up one finger to make his point. 'I mean a funny-peculiar . . . not funny-ha-ha . . . if you get me.'

'I dig you all right . . .' Adam joked back.

He was surprised to find that as each day passed, and he adapted himself to this new life, he was enjoying it. He liked getting to know his patients well, having them talk of other things, perhaps ask his advice on some family argument. In Durban, he and the other junior partners had had no personal patients, they had merely stood in for the senior doctors when necessary. It had been much more impersonal than this sort of general practice. Durban was a big city and the group of doctors had a great many patients so that it was a rare thing for the junior doctors ever to know any individual patient well.

He left the hospital earlier than usual one morning and had half an hour before he was to open his town surgery. It was a perfect December day. Hot, of course, but with a pleasant mountain breeze. The town was full of shoppers, mostly Africans, many in their vividly-coloured tribal clothes, many others in smart suits and short skirted elegant frocks. He knew if he went into the surgery Mrs. Platt would make him a cup of coffee but something made him hesitate on the pavement.

It was then he saw Charon.

She was hurrying along the road, her head bent. She was wearing white shorts and a white shirt and he wondered what the Sisters at the Hospital would have said had they seen her.

He walked to meet her. 'Charon . . .' he began.

She stopped dead, her head jerked back and for a moment she stared at him blankly. Then her long dark eyelashes flickered as she recognised him.

'Dr. Bray . . .' she said and smiled.

'Adam, please . . .' he told her. 'We don't go in for formalities up here. How are things?'

'Fine, just fine,' she said quickly and then she half-closed her eyes. 'Well, they're not too bad,' she added.

'Come and have coffee and tell me about it,'

he said, taking her arm.

'Well . . . I . . . Robin brought me down and . . .'

'He'll find you. We've only one café . . .'

Holding her arm firmly, he led the way to the one small restaurant. The walls were painted cream, blue and pink, there was soft music from a hidden recorder, and at the moment, they were the only customers. He chose a table in the window so that she would relax and not keep looking for her brother. He had a feeling that it might help her to be able to talk to someone.

Charon did not seem to need much persuasion before she began talking. It reminded Adam of a pressure cooker letting off steam. As if she had stifled it for so long that it had to explode.

'It would be all right if only she wouldn't keep talking about it . . . .' Charon said, looking down at the pattern she was drawing on the cloth with the prongs of a fork. 'She just won't let up . . .' she went on, her voice soft and restrained. 'She keeps talking about it and asking me questions. Was I treated well at the Orphanage. Did I have enough to eat. Did they give us birthday presents. Could we have parties . . . then she talks about . . . about the Webbs. Were they old or young. What sort of life did we lead. Did I have a good chance of education. Had I any idea of what career I would like . . . and then it starts again: was I very lonely, did I wish I was like other girls with parents to love me.' Charon lifted her head and looked at Adam and he was shocked by the utter misery he saw in her eyes.

'If only she would stop,' Charon went on desperately. 'I don't want to hurt her. She's so nice. You can't help liking her. If she asks me if I was happy at the Orphanage, I never seem to have the right answer. If I say I wasn't . . . and I wasn't always . . . but then no one is ever always happy, are they? I mean, if I say I wasn't, then I see her close her eyes and I know she's trying not to cry, but if I tell her I was happy, she looks at me and I know she doesn't believe me. She thinks I'm telling her to make her feel better.'

'I'm afraid she has to punish herself,' Adam said slowly.

'But she's also punishing me,' Charon cried. 'You can't think how awful it is.'

She twisted her hands together miserably and looked down at them.

'She's not like that with Robin . . .'

'But then Robin's life has been quite different. He's been happily adopted for his whole life. She feels far more guilt because of you, Charon.'

Charon looked up. 'But it really wasn't her fault, was it?'

Adam noted the 'really' and stifled a sigh.

'I mean, she did her best to get us adopted together. It was my fault for being a delicate

84

baby . . .'

Adam laughed. 'Honestly Charon . . .'

She laughed as well. 'I know. I sound almost hysterical but honestly, Doc . . . I mean . . . I mean, Adam . . .' She said the name slowly, looking at him. 'Adam. It's rather a nice name. D'you like it?'

The waitress brought them the coffee and he ordered chocolate cakes.

'Not as much as I like Charon. D'you like that?'

'I prefer it to Girlie . . .' she said.

'It's funny what trouble parents always seem to have about names. They try to please relations . . .'

'I've known lots of girls who've hated their names . . .'

'Yes, and I've known lots of boys who've had ridiculous names. I must say I got ragged a lot at school about my name but I early learned to be aggressive.'

Charon laughed outright. 'That I can't believe. You—aggressive? Never.'

He was startled. 'I can be . . .'

'Perhaps. If it was really necessary . . .'

He felt suddenly uncomfortable. 'How d'you get on with the Lillingtons?' he asked, seizing the chance to change the subject.

Her face clouded over. 'Oh, all right. Mr. Lillington I like very much. He reminds me of Daddy . . . I mean of Mr. Webb. Mr. Lillington makes me feel . . . well, sort of protected. And

85

he's good to me, too. Know what? He's going to teach me to drive a car.' For a moment her eyes shone. 'He's even said one day he'll let me drive his tractor. We get on well.' She laughed. 'They've got a wonderful sort of game, you drive model cars by remote control and we're always having races. I often win . . .'

'And the young ones?'

Her happiness seemed to vanish. 'They're all right . . .' She looked at her hands thoughtfully and then gave the movement he was beginning to expect as she lifted her head abruptly and looked into his eyes. 'Quite honestly, I'm not with it, as Pippa would put it. I always feel outside. Robin fits in well. He loves riding. They've got four horses, you know. I can't ride. I don't want to. I'm not all that fond of animals. The same with the dogs. They're all right . . . I suppose. I'm just not used to dogs licking my face and nearly knocking me over.' She gave an uneasy laugh. 'I try to pretend I don't mind but . . .'

'You're easily scared, aren't you,' Adam said quietly.

She looked startled. 'Yes, I'm afraid I'm a coward.'

'Oh, no you're not,' Adam said, his voice sharp. 'On the contrary. If you were, you'd scream when one of the dogs came near you. The fact that you pretend to like them shows what courage you've got . . .'

Charon looked startled. 'Does it? I never

86

thought of it that way ...'

'Well, think of it, Charon. It's time you got some self-confidence, faith in yourself. How d'you get on with the kids on the whole?'

'I'm accepted but I don't fit in. Except with Keith. He's teaching me to play chess. I didn't think boys as young as he could play. Oh, and Midge. I adore her.' Charon's eyes shone. 'Jeremy ignores me. He's at the age when boys pretend they despise girls.'

He glanced at his watch and caught his breath with dismay.

'Help! I'm late. Mrs. Platt will slay me. I'd no idea it was so late ...'

Charon leaned forward to look at his watch and gasped. 'It can't be ...' She looked up at him. 'It's funny how you can talk to some people and not to others, isn't it? I can talk to Robin about anything, and to Aunt Irene and to Mr. Lillington and ... and to you ...'

He looked down into her eyes. 'I expect it's because I'm a doctor, Charon,' he said gently. 'A sort of impersonal ear to pour your troubles into. Doctors are like priests in that respect. Part of our work is to listen. Now, try not to worry and just live each day as it comes. Eleanor will soon lose this painful sense of guilt that compels her to probe and hurt herself. I'm sure everything will be all right.'

Charon stood up. 'Thanks for the coffee and ... and for everything. I hope things will turn out all right. I'd hate to hurt her.'

Adam paid the check and turned back to the waiting girl.

'I'm sure they will, Charon,' he said quietly. 'You see I know you. Probably better than you know yourself so I'm certain everything will be all right.'

CHAPTER NINE

Charon stood on the pavement and watched Adam hurry away. She kept remembering what he'd said: 'You see I know you—probably better than you know yourself . . .'

What a strange thing for him to say when they'd only met twice. Well, three times, if you could include that brief moment in the hospital in Durban.

She walked down the street, past groups of Africans lounging outside a shop and chatting, sometimes bursting into laughter, past girls pushing prams proudly, mothers clambering out of cars, closing the doors firmly on children and dogs who wanted to join them.

Everywhere there was movement and colour, she thought. Used to life in busy Durban, she found this quieter way of living fascinating. She now knew so many people but she still felt shy when they stopped to speak to her. Now she saw Robin hurrying towards her, waving frantically.

He was breathless when he reached her, and apologetic.

'Sorry I was so long, Charon, but I got caught up with some old schoolfriends and we had to have a drink.' He grinned. 'Hope you weren't worried about me?'

'Of course not. I was afraid you'd be worried about me,' Charon laughed. 'I met the doctor . . . Adam, I mean, and we had coffee together.'

Robin gave her a strange look. 'You like him? Seems a bit square to me . . .'

'Oh, Robin . . .' Charon laughed again. 'Of course he isn't. It's just that he's older than we are and takes life seriously.'

'So do you, poppet, far too seriously . . .' Robin took her hand and walked with her to his M.G. 'I've promised Ma to pick up the groceries, she phoned down an order, and I've got to get the meat for the dogs. Okay?'

Charon settled herself comfortably into the seat and smiled.

'Anything you say, Robin. I'm in your hands.'

For once, she felt really happy. Robin, at least, loved her and went out of his way to help her adjust herself to this strange new life. Adam, too, liked her and his words which she kept repeating to herself silently, were another comfort. Everything would work out all right, he'd promised her, and said he knew that because he knew her better than she knew herself.

He'd said another thing. He'd told her that she was brave and not a coward. Yet she was afraid of many things. Emotional scenes such as . . . as her real mother seemed to love, or, if she didn't like them, seemed determined to create them. Then she was scared of being ducked. She loathed her face going under water. She was scared, too, of the big dogs who were so boisterously loving.

After Robin had picked up the shopping and was driving towards the Lillingtons' farm, Charon said abruptly:

'Are you frightened of anything, Robin?'

He was startled, turned to look at her. 'Of course I am. Scared stiff of many things.'

'Such as?' Charon found it hard to believe him.

'Such as . . .? Well, marriage.' Robin frowned as he stared ahead. The road wound and cattle had an unhappy knack of straying across the road, unattended, so if you took a corner too fast, you could find yourself in the midst of a herd. Or goats who had a habit of suddenly jumping down the rocky steep hillsides and leisurely crossing the road, every now and then turning heads to sneer at the impatient drivers.

'Yes, marriage,' he went on thoughtfully. 'A lot of students I know, Charon, are married. It doesn't work. Perhaps once in a hundred. They usually get jobs in the holidays but it

90

doesn't bring in enough if the wife has to give up work and have a baby. That's what floors them every time.'

'But you're only scared of marriage as a student?'

'No, not only. Seems to me marriage is a terrific step to take. Instantly you're tied. Your freedom curtailed. You have to think of someone else. Maybe I'm selfish but I've a career ahead of me and I don't want to get caught up. Another thing, Charon, all this . . .' He waved a hand vaguely. 'This business about children and adoptions and all that—scares me stiff. How can you be sure you're doing the right thing? Ma was given advice by her doctor and she followed it. I can imagine how difficult it must have been . . .'

'You're more understanding than I am, Robin. I . . . I just can't see how she could have parted with us . . .'

He glanced at her. 'That's because you've never had a sick husband and twins who never stop screaming and one who may die at any moment. The poor kid must have been nearly out of her mind.'

'I wish I could feel that way but . . .'

Robin swung the car through the white gates. 'That's understandable, Charon. You and I've had such different lives. Now if the Webbs were still alive and Ma had turned up like this, you'd have rushed at her with open arms and all would be well. But you can't help blaming her for your misery after the Webbs died. Misery that certainly wasn't her fault . . .'

'I know . . .' Charon said unhappily. 'I do like her, Robin. I think she's very nice but . . .'

He parked the car under the thatched roof of the carport. And patted her hand. 'Not to worry, Charon. It'll work out all right. Don't worry,' he told her.

The dogs came rushing, leaping up and Charon stayed in the car, pretending to fumble with her handbag until their first exuberance had sobered down. Even then they came to her side, jumping up, and she had to force herself to pat them and smile. There seemed so many of them.

There was Jock, a Great Dane, Liz a big Dalmatian, Phooey, a plump little dachshund and Mickey, a fox terrier. They adored the children and followed them everywhere.

Now Pippa came round the house, in white shorts and a striped shirt.

'At last, Robin . . .' she shouted. 'You promised to play tennis with me.'

'Help. Sorry. I forgot. See you . . .' Robin grinned at Charon, yelled at the housegirl to bring in the shopping and was off, the dogs leaping and barking as they followed him round the corner of the house.

Charon quietly slipped into the house and to her room. She stood at the window, gazing out. The house was big but the two younger children were now sharing a room so that she could have Keith's, and Robin was sharing a room with Jeremy.

Charon could see the neat rows of citrus trees marching up the hillside behind, could glimpse the swimming pool and the tennis court where Robin was already playing tennis with Pippa. If only, Charon thought miserably, she was like Robin. If only she could play tennis and ride and swim well, so that the children could accept her and not leave her 'outside'.

She stayed in her room until lunch time and then when she joined the others and they asked her what she had been doing, she told a half-lie and said she'd been writing letters. It was not the complete truth for she had only started a letter to dear old Mrs. Jugg, who must be longing to know how they were getting on, since she remembered the name of the country 'Amanzi' their mother had come from.

But what could she say? That everything was lovely when it wasn't? Or the truth that she was on edge all the time lest her real mother start asking questions and showing so plainly her feelings of guilt for having had the twins adopted? That she loved her real mother? That was a lie. She liked her, yes. Admired, her, too, but . . .

So she had torn up the stiffly-worded letter she'd begun and decided to send Mrs. Jugg a postcard instead.

They had lunch out on the wide stoep, the

sun hot, the garden bright with flowering bushes for, like most farmers, Sam Lillington felt that the ground was there for farming and not for flowers!

'I do hope you two will stay for Christmas?' Eleanor Lillington said in a carefully casual voice that failed to fool Charon. She glanced up quickly and met her mother's eyes, saw the appeal in them, and felt a bit sick with misery.

'Oh, yes, Robin . . . do . . .' Pippa said quickly, tossing back her long red hair.

'Yes, do.' Jeremy agreed, looking at Robin.

Keith smiled shyly at Charon, though. Will you? he mouthed the words silently. They had a little game they played, they were learning to lip-read and, at Keith's suggestion, had sent away for books to teach them how to learn the deaf and dumb way of talking by signs. Keith, apparently, had been very moved by a talk at school regarding a book written about a deaf and dumb child who could not communicate with anyone, because she couldn't read or write, and to Keith it had seemed quite frightening.

'We might meet someone like that one day, Charon,' he'd said, his young face worried. 'And we'd feel awful if we couldn't help them, wouldn't we?'

She'd agreed, so it was their secret.

'I don't know . . .' she mouthed back.

Robin was the first to speak. He looked embarrassed.

'It's very sweet of you, Ma, and I'm sure Charon and I would love it but there's Mum. You see, Christmas means an awful lot to her. Since Dad died . . . well, I'm all she's got. I couldn't just walk out and leave her alone . . .'

Eleanor leaned forward eagerly. 'Of course not. Let's ask her, too, shall we?'

Charon felt herself relax. She liked 'Aunt Irene' very much and knew that having her here would cause the tense atmosphere to relax.

'That would be lovely,' Charon said impulsively and saw her mother's instant relief.

'I'll write to her today, Robin . . .'

'Goody, goody,' Pippa said briskly. 'Now that's settled, Robin, what about a ride this afternoon? We could go up Angel's Peak and . . .'

Robin looked at Charon enquiringly. 'Got any plans?' he asked.

Charon saw Pippa's quick frown of annoyance and smiled at Robin. 'Keith and I have plans,' Charon said.

Keith reacted instantly. 'That's right . . .' he said and looked at Charon and mouthed the words: 'That's fine with me. What shall we do?'

She mouthed back silently: 'If the others all go riding, let's swim'.

He grinned in agreement and they all separated. It was a pleasant afternoon for Charon. She and Keith swam leisurely together, floating on a lilo and talking. He wanted to know what life was like in an orphanage—'just in case' he explained, but somehow his questions didn't hurt Charon as his mother's questions did, She tried to draw as truthful a picture as possible, showing him it was like permanent boarding school. She left out the bits she'd hated, the sharing of your possessions, the fact that you weren't allowed to keep your own toys, be an individual, and the awfulness, to her, at least, of belonging to no one.

'I'm never going to have children . . .' Keith announced suddenly.

Charon turned her head to look at the nine-year-old boy.

'Why ever not?'

'Just in case I die and they have to be orphans.'

'Oh but Keith . . . if everyone thought that then there'd be no people in the world. It isn't everyone minds being an orphan. Your father was one, wasn't he? Who looked after him?'

'He was lucky. A friend of his father's, and then he got married so Dad did have sort of parents. Are you going to have children?'

Charon trailed her hand in the lukewarm water and gazed up at the blue cloudless sky thoughtfully. 'Know something, Keith, I've never thought about it.'

'You must have . . .' Keith said firmly. 'That's all girls talk about. Getting a husband

and having children.'

Charon smiled at his tone of authority. 'Well, maybe I have thought that one day I might meet a very nice man and get married . . .'

'See . . .' Keith said triumphantly.

'Children? Yes, Keith, I would like children. At least, four and if possible six.'

He whistled softly. 'And if everyone had eight children and then died, think how full the orphanages would be . . .'

'Oh, Keith . . .' Charon began to laugh. 'You're the end, really . . .' Suddenly she heard a horse neighing. 'Sounds like they're back, Keith. I'm getting out . . .'

'Me, too,' he said, both rolled over and into the water, swimming quickly to the side so that they had rubbed themselves dry and were lying in the sun before Robin and Pippa came round the corner.

'Hey, lazy things . . .' Robin said. 'How about a swim? We're going to . . .'

Charon blinked at him sleepily. 'We've been swimming all afternoon, thanks.'

'Okay . . . okay . . .' Robin said agreeably and hurried into the house to change, Pippa close behind him.

Charon turned her head and smiled at Keith. He grinned back. They both felt the same and, oddly enough, could admit it to the other without shame. When Robin and Pippa swam, Keith and Charon manoeuvred things so that they stayed out of the water. Neither had ever mentioned it but they worked as a team, helping one another, recognising but not admitting that they each were scared.

*   *   *

Irene Mortlake's answer came by return of post.

'I'd love to come. Robin seems to be having a wonderful time and I'd hate to spoil his holiday.'

Christmas was approaching with speed. Sam brought home a tall Christmas tree he'd got from the local forestry officer and Eleanor got out her boxes of decorations and they all set to work. Charon worried about presents. She had little money for she had spent what 'Aunt Irene' had given her and one day, she was startled when opening her handbag to find ten one dollar notes in it.

'How on earth . . . .' Charon began and looked up to see her mother gazing anxiously at her.

'Please, Charon,' she said softly. 'There's so little I can do . . .'

A strange feeling filled Charon. She saw the misery in her mother's eyes, the appeal and she moved impulsively, putting her arms round her mother, kissing her cheek.

'Thanks a ton. You're doing a lot . . .' She stood back, embarrassed for it was the first time she had kissed her mother.

Then she saw the happiness on her mother's face, the way the lines had vanished as she smiled.

'Thanks,' Charon repeated. 'Now I can have fun and buy presents.'

'If you want any more, please ask for it . . .' Eleanor Lillington said, her voice nervous.

Charon smiled at her. A big warm smile that delighted Eleanor. 'I will, Ma . . .' Charon said, the word coming with surprising ease to her lips, 'I promise.'

CHAPTER TEN

Eleanor Lillington invited Adam to spend Christmas Day with them. His parents urged him to do so.

'Be a change for you, Adam,' his mother said slowly. 'You're working too hard.'

'But it's the first Christmas I've been home for years,' he began.

His mother laughed. 'If you're anything like your father and have his bad luck, most of your Christmas Day will be spent at the hospital or visiting houses. Go and enjoy yourself, Adam dear. We'll see you in the evening.'

So he had accepted the invitation, reminding Eleanor that 'anything' could happen and not to count on him.

'I need your help, Adam,' Eleanor told him quietly.

Christmas Day hadn't started too well. He'd gone down to the brightly decorated hospital, gone to the small ward for children and found that several new cases with nasty burns had been brought in and, just before he left, two casualties came in requiring a cast of one arm and six stitches in the head of another. But at last, he left the hospital, telling them he'd be at the Lillingtons.

The big white house was gay with life and laughter, cars parked in the drive. He walked round the house and saw that they were all sitting on the patio.

Charon saw him first and jumped up impulsively.

'Happy Christmas, Adam . . .' she said gaily.

'Happy Christmas . . .' He smiled down at her—but not very far down for she was an extraordinarily tall girl. 'Hope I'm not late.'

'We understood, anyhow. Come and meet Aunt Irene . . .' Charon said. 'This is Robin's adoptive mother,' she said softly to Adam.

He was interested in meeting Irene Mortlake and he liked what he saw, for the short, plumpish, elegantly-dressed woman had a warm smile and affectionate eyes as she spoke to Charon.

Soon he was engulfed in the family rejoicings, opening a parcel for him from Charon of a very elegant silk tie, wishing he'd thought to bring her a present. The children were wild with delight, the little 'monster' as the youngest was called, riding up and down on her tiny rocking-horse with shouts of glee. Pippa, horse mad, had been given so many books on horses that he wondered if she'd ever read them all! She also had been given some elegant riding boots and a new saddle. Jeremy had a new bicycle, Keith a chess set which he showed everyone proudly.

'It's a travelling set,' he explained patiently to Adam, opening the zip-fastened case and showing the small ivory men. 'Now Charon and I can play it by the pool without bringing everything out.'

'You and Charon play chess?' Adam asked.

Keith nodded. 'I taught her. She's quite good. For a girl.'

Adam nodded, trying not to smile. 'You get on with her?'

'With Charon? Of course. She's the nicest sister I've got . . .'

Adam was pleased to hear that but he noticed for himself what Charon had told him that day they'd sat and talked and drank coffee. Charon was not 'in' with the other children, at least, not with Pippa and Jeremy who devoted all their attention to Robin.

Seizing the chance to talk to Charon alone, Adam walked with her to the paddock where there were four horses.

'You don't ride?' he said casually.

She gave a little shiver and turned to him. 'Don't tell a soul but I'm terrified of horses.' She smiled. 'I know it sounds ridiculous but . . .'

'I don't think so. I've known men faint at the sight of a needle.'

'A needle?' She looked shocked.

He smiled. 'A hypodermic needle, I mean, for giving shots. Then I've known people run at the sight of a spider so you're not so very different from the normal person.'

She laughed. 'Thanks. You're so comforting.'

He looked at her. She was wearing a pale yellow frock, a very great deal shorter than the navy blue frock she'd worn that first time he saw her. He thought suddenly—and rather to his surprise—that in her own way, Charon was beautiful. Those dark eyes that suddenly blazed and the next moment were demure and half-hidden by long dark lashes. The high cheekbones, exaggerated by the short hair cut. Her slender legs.

'Enjoying yourself?' he asked casually.

She turned to him, her face flushed. 'Oh, so much, Adam, I don't ever remember a Christmas like this. Even with the Webbs, there were just the three of us. No other people. And now Aunt Irene has come, everything is much easier.'

'It is?'

She hesitated. 'Well . . . in a way, it takes . . .

takes Ma off my back.'

Adam caught his breath and kept his face impassive. So Charon had overcome one of the greatest obstacles before her and had found it possible to call Eleanor 'Ma' as Robin did. That was a big step forward, he thought, absurdly pleased.

'How?' he asked casually.

'Well, they talk a lot together. Ma hasn't so much time to worry about me. She's always so afraid I'm not happy and she really is most generous. If only . . .'

'If only?' he echoed quietly.

He saw Charon's hands gripping the top rail of the paddock, saw how white her knuckles showed through the taut skin.

'If only I could understand . . .' she said slowly. 'I just can't imagine . . .' She turned to him, her eyes imploring for help, 'how any mother could let her children go.'

'But being brought up—or at least for eleven years—in an orphanage, surely this is something you should be able to accept. The fact is that, although you can't *understand* it, mothers do give up the children they love. Isn't the fault perhaps in yourself, Charon? I mean, what right have you to judge unless you've been in similar circumstances?'

'I know. I know. You're so right. That's just what Robin says to me . . .' Charon ran an agonised hand through her hair so that it stuck up all round in little points. Which Adam, to his amazement, found rather endearing. 'But I can't . . .'

'At least you call her Ma. That must please her.'

He watched her flush. 'Yes. I'm glad I can but . . .'

'We'd better go back or they'll send out a search party,' Adam said, taking Charon's arm. 'Not to worry as I said before. Time straightens out a lot of things.'

'But I feel so mean . . . and so awfully ungrateful and I absolutely hate her being hurt. It's just . . .'

Adam patted her hand. 'Let's leave it at that,' he said gently. 'You're doing fine.'

Eleanor was looking for them and came to meet them.

'The others are going to swim, Adam. Want to join them?'

He shook his head. 'I'd rather sit and relax . . .'

'Chary . . . Chary . . .' small Midge was screaming. 'I want Chary . . .'

Midge, the little 'Monster', was wearing a miniature bikini and she held out her hands to Charon.

'You take me in, Chary. I likes going in with you . . .' she commanded.

'Come with me while I change,' Charon said, with a backward smile at Adam, and hurried into the house with the small plump four-year old hurrying after her.

104

'There's a shady seat up here,' Eleanor said, leading Adam up one of the few paths that went through the citrus trees so near the pool. They came to a clearing with a huge old oak tree, round whose trunk had been built a bench.

'Not very comfy but adequate for the short while we've got,' Eleanor said.

He gave her a cigarette, lit it, and then lit one for himself. Still, Eleanor said nothing. She sat by his side, staring into space. Phooey, the dachshund, had followed her and now climbed up onto her lap. She scratched behind his ear, her mind obviously occupied.

'You wanted my help?' Adam said quietly.

Eleanor nodded. 'Yes. D'you think Charon is still suffering from shock? Shock at the news, I mean.'

Adam considered the question carefully, watching her face which had lost all its happiness as she spoke.

'I'd say she is slowly recovering from the shock. She's beginning to adjust and accept things that before, her mind blocked and refused to accept. If you get me?'

'I think so. Things are much better, of course. There is no longer that . . . that rejection of me she showed at first, no longer that look as if I was some monster . . .' Eleanor smiled unsteadily. 'Things are very much better but . . .'

'I think it causes Charon as much sorrow as

it does you, Eleanor. She's trying so hard to love you . . .'

Startled, Eleanor faced him. 'Does she have to try hard?'

He nodded. 'Don't forget that your maternal love is deeply ingrained in you. But the same thing does not apply to a child. Maternal love is designed for protection and is a totally different kind of love. A child's love demands protection, security and love . . .'

'All the things I denied her,' Eleanor said bitterly.

He turned to look at her. 'Eleanor, you're not helping Charon or yourself by this . . . this constant self-flagellation. I'm sure you did what you thought best . . .'

'The doctor advised it . . .'

'I know. Your husband was, I gathered . . .'

'Sick. Very sick,' Eleanor said quickly.

'Your family wouldn't help? Hadn't your husband any relations?'

'He had a father and a sister but they strongly disapproved of me and told Tim not to come crawling for help when we needed it. Tim would have died rather than go to them, besides he wasn't . . .' She stopped abruptly. 'My parents might have helped us, though I'd have hated to ask them. They also strongly disapproved of Tim and said we were stupid fools to marry. But I think when things were so bad, I'd have gone to them only they were on a tour round the world. A trip they never came

106

back from. Their ship was in a collision and their bodies never found.'

'They left you no money?'

'A little . . . but by the time they died and I knew what money I was going to get, it was too late. The children had been adopted. As I thought, by one lot of parents.'

'I honestly don't see what else you could have done,' Adam began but Eleanor looked at him.

'I know what I should have done. Swallowed my pride and crawled to Tim's sister. I'm not even sure she'd have helped us then but I would feel better now, if I had tried it . . .'

There was a sudden hooting of horns and Eleanor jumped up.

'We've got some friends coming and it must be time to eat . . . Come on . . .'

She led the way. Adam was introduced to two rather elderly white-haired people and to their grand-daughter, a very attractive girl in her teens with blonde hair and very short skirts. Adam noticed the way the girl's eyes flickered over him and the way she said:

'You're a doctor? I'm studying medicine, myself,' and then the way she looked at Robin as he came up out of the pool to be introduced, his long black curly hair dripping water, his sun-tanned broad shoulders impressive as he smiled at her.

'You're studying law?' the girl said and laughed. 'Oh, what a bind. At least we have fun, we do things . . .'

'So do we . . .' Robin laughed.

Dinner was a fantastic meal and Adam wondered how many servants Eleanor had, or if she was merely an extraordinarily good organiser, for the meal was perfect. All the traditional dishes despite the blazing sunshine. Turkey and cranberry sauce. Christmas pudding ablaze with lighted brandy. Mince pies. Ice cream. They all ate off their laps, squatting down on the grass or on chairs, all talking and laughing. Adam managed to join Charon's group which included Keith and Midge and was amused, and rather startled, by Keith's comments and also noticed that the instant Pippa, Jeremy or Robin joined their group, Kieth shut up like a clam and retreated into his normal shell of a shy, rather stupid boy.

In the middle of it, Adam was sent for. This was a surgical case and the doctor on duty had his hands full already as there had been a bus accident.

Everyone sympathised and Adam felt quite sorry to leave the friendly throng. He was rather surprised at this reaction because normally he was not the social type and rarely went out to parties. But then Adam was being surprised recently about many things that affected him. He was changing in many ways . . . almost as though he was seeing the world with new eyes.

Once at the hospital he had no time to think. His first patient was a girl in her teens. He examined her quickly, noting the rapid pulse, how wet and clammy her skin was and how her eyes showed the pain. He discovered a marked tenderness at a point between the hip and the umbillicus and he turned quickly to the Sister by his side, giving instructions.

Much later, he hung the film on the rack and turned to face the parents of another patient, a small boy, this time.

'He was born with his hip out of joint. This can be corrected by an operation. We'll need to keep him here under observation . . .'

The mother, a middle-aged African woman, wept bitterly but the husband's face was stoic.

'We had six children,' he said. 'They all died but this, who is our last. Must he also die?'

Adam shook his head violently. 'Most certainly not but you want him to walk like other boys? Then he must be left with us . . .'

An African nurse in a butcher blue frock and a starched apron and cap led the parents away. Adam gave another look at the frightened dark face of the boy in bed and gave him a sweet.

'Not to worry, kid,' he said gently. 'We'll find a way.'

The reception-desk nurse called him.

'There's been a fire in the Lawsons' house, sir, and the two children are slightly burned but badly shocked. It might be better to go over than bring them here . . .'

'I agree,' Adam said, taking off his white cap and removing the gauze mask. 'Let's see . . . where do the Lawsons live?'

The girl told him and he drove straight to the house. One side of it was badly charred, smoke slowly spiralling. The fire engine was there—firemen standing around, a dribbling hose in hand, some of them chatting. A policeman came to Adam's side.

'The parents are out, celebrating, no doubt. We're trying to find them. The kids are really creating, poor little blighters.'

Adam walked into the house, following the sound of screaming. The nursery was easily found. In the cot, a year old boy was jumping up and down, screaming his head off. On the floor, a three year old boy sat, banging his head hard against the wall in a strangely rhythmic manner.

Adam had a look at the smallest one who screamed even louder while the older boy banged his head harder. Adam had an idea. Went in search of and found the telephone. He phoned the Lillingtons. Spoke to the housegirl and asked for Miss Charon.

In a moment he was telling Charon all about it. 'I can't cope with the two on my own. Think you could come and lend a hand?'

'Of course. Where are you? The Lawsons? I'll get Robin to run me over . . .' Charon promised.

Adam returned to the children, picked up the boy from the floor and he went absolutely rigid in Adam's arms.

He heard the car stop. Robin must have driven at a terrific rate, Adam thought, and then Charon was there. She took in the situation at a glance and lifted the rigid child from Adam's arms.

'We had one like this at the hospital,' she said, her voice calm. 'It's only shock, isn't it?'

He nodded, opening his case to get out the needed instruments.

Robin was in the doorway. 'I gather they can't find the Lawsons,' he said. 'So I'm going to look for them.'

'Thanks.' Adam said, not looking up as he gave the stiff child an injection.

Charon sat on the floor, holding the body tightly, rocking herself slowly backwards and forwards, talking softly, and gradually the rigidness seemed to go and the stiff body became a small boy again, rounded, warm, but still unconscious.

Adam was examining the smaller child, who was still screaming a little but sounding sleepier because of the drug injected, for burns.

'I don't think the fire reached them,' he said. 'Probably smoke and the sound . . . then the fire engine screaming up and they thought all the devils from hell were after them . . .'

There was the screech of tyres and a man

and a woman came hurrying into the room.

Charon recognised Leila Lawson vaguely. She'd seen her in town and had also heard she was a bridge fiend.

'My babies,' Leila cried. 'What have you done to them?' She snatched the child from Charon and almost screamed. 'He's unconscious . . . Is he in a coma?'

The man, tall, with a rather aggressive moustache wanted to know what had happened. 'Can't we go out for a few hours . . .'

'I know nothing,' Adam said, straightening his aching back. 'Simply that I was sent for. Better see the police . . . they've been looking for you . . .'

'Well, that's absurd . . . the girl could have told them,' the man blustered angrily. 'We gave her the phone number and . . .'

'Where is the girl?' Leila Lawson asked.

'I gathered there was no one here when the police came . . .'

'But how did it happen?' Harold Lawson demanded.

Adam looked at him wearily. 'How do I know? It's your house, your fire and your children. They're both in a state of shock . . .'

Leila began to cry. 'She seemed a good girl. I thought we could trust her for a few hours.'

'Have you had her long?' Adam asked.

Leila looked up. 'No, only a week but she seemed all right . . . The children always slept when I put them to bed and . . .'

At last Adam and Charon got away. Robin was waiting outside in the car.

'Sorry to drag you away from the party,' Adam said as he opened the door of the car and waited while Charon got in. 'Thanks for coming to help, Charon. I couldn't have managed alone.'

'Thanks for asking me, Adam,' she said quickly. 'Any time, you know. I'm used to helping out in hospital . . .'

He lifted his hand in farewell.

'Adam . . .' Charon called and Robin braked so that Adam could catch up with them and stand by Charon's side of the car, looking down at her. 'Adam—you know what you said to me once about mothers being born mothers. I don't think that one was. How could she leave her two children alone with a housegirl she hardly knew? Wasn't that dreadful of her? I don't know how any decent . . .'

'Charon . . .' Adam's voice was gentle but he was overwhelmingly tired all of a sudden. 'Try to remember that you were brought up in an atmosphere where black was black and white was white. I'm talking about right and wrong not skins,' he added. 'What I'm trying to get through to you is the fact that there are many shades of grey. If Leila had insisted on staying at home, her husband would have gone to the party alone. He shouldn't, I agree . . .' He spoke quickly as she began to interrupt. 'But

113

he would have. Many a mother has to make a choice. To smother her children with love and protect them every hour of their lives or to be a real wife, in other words, a companion to her husband. When a man marries, he marries a woman. Not a mother. It was just very unfortunate that the girl they employed was not to be trusted. On a hundred similar occasions, probably even a thousand, all would have been well. Charon, you're young. Don't jump to conclusions and damn people before you know all the facts of the case. It was unwise to leave those two children with an unknown housegirl but no real damage has been done and Leila Lawson will never forgive herself. Isn't that punishment enough without you passing judgement on her? I must go . . .'

He walked away fast to his car. Had he spoken too harshly to Charon, he wondered. Yet this intolerant attitude of hers alarmed him. It wasn't in keeping with her nature. She was a nice girl, compassionate but not understanding. Would she ever grow out of it, he wondered.

Back at the hospital, there were more casualties waiting. He put on his white overall and began to work, forgetting everything else.

CHAPTER ELEVEN

Charon half-opened her eyes sleepily as she heard the soft familiar voice.

'You are waked up, aren't you, Chary?' it said. 'You are waked up? Mummy said not to talk till you're waked . . .'

Charon knew she should be used to Midge's daily onslaught but she always had to fight to wake up.

'Yes, I'm waked up . . .' she said in the middle of a big yawn.

'I'm so cold, Chary, can I come into bed with you?' Midge went on. Which was absurd, of course, for early though it was, the sun was already hot, but Midge's formula musn't be disturbed.

'Of course, darling . . .' Charon yawned again and lifted the sheet which was all the bed-clothing she needed.

Midge, in her shortie pyjamas crept into bed and nestled close to her. 'You will stay for ever, won't you, Chary?'

'For ever's a long time, Midge,' Charon said, cuddling the small girl. 'You'll be grown up by then and a great actress and . . .'

Midge looked at her with her huge, appealing eyes.

'You really fink I will be a great actress?'

'I'm sure you'll be a great something.'

'What's a something?'

Charon stifled a smile. Midge's dignity was easily hurt! 'A something is something that isn't a nothing.'

'And what's a nothing?'

'A nothing is something that isn't a something,' Charon said gravely.

Midge beamed. 'And I'm a Something?'

She was silent for a moment or two while Charon drifted off into a half-doze, broken by Midge's voice again:

'I want you to stay for ever, Chary, 'cos I like you the best of all.'

'Thanks, darling,' Charon said sleepily but flattered. 'Why?'

' 'Cos you don't tease me and you always do what I say.'

Charon's smile was wry. Maybe she was spoiling Midge. It was hard not to when a child was such a darling but perhaps Mother Superior would take a different view!

'And you never ever get cross,' Midge went on.

Charon laughed. 'Oh, I do! Sometimes. But not with you.'

'I'se never seen you cross.'

'I hide it in here . . .' Charon tapped her body.

'In your tummy?' Midge's eyes widened. 'That's where babies come from. Have you got a baby in there?' she asked solemnly.

It was all Charon could do not to laugh. The

116

questions kids think up!

'No, Midge darling.'

Midge looked quite offended. 'Why not? Wouldn't you like a baby?'

'Because I'm not married.'

'Why not?'

Midge made it sound so simple, Charon thought, amused, but she kept her voice grave as she answered.

'Because I'm not in love with someone. You don't get married if you don't meet someone whom you love.'

'What is love?'

Charon frowned thoughtfully. How could you define love, she wondered. Especially so that a child of four could understand.

'Loving is wanting to make a person happy,' Charon said slowly. 'Wanting to be with them all the time. Being happy when you're with them. Wanting to help them . . .'

'Then I'm in love with you,' Midge said triumphantly. 'Can we get married and then we'll have lots of babies and . . .'

'I'm afraid you're a girl and girls marry men . . .'

Midge made a grimace. 'Like Keith and Jeremy and . . . Robin? I wouldn't mind Robin . . .'

'You couldn't marry any of them because they're your brothers.'

'Why not . . . ?'

Charon drew a deep breath. Things were

getting too involved. 'Because it's against the law. How about a swim before breakfast, Midge? Race you to the bathroom . . .'

Midge forget everything else with a shriek of delight as she tumbled out of bed.

'I get there first . . .' she shouted.

She did. But then, she always did! Maybe, Charon thought, she shouldn't let Midge always win. It wasn't easy always to do the right thing with a child.

The day that began with a perfect sunrise changed in mid-afternoon. They were sitting by the pool, all talking, the strains of Pippa's favourite pop tunes coming from the stables for she carried her favourite Christmas present of a small transistor radio with her everywhere. Dark clouds were massing in the sky, moving fast towards them and suddenly they heard a distant roar, like the sound of an advancing and enormous swarm of angry bees and everyone jumped up, and ran to the house but the rain beat them to it, moving up the valley with surprising force, the air was suddenly grey with rain and they were all stumbling, laughing, drenched to the skin.

Charon stood in the lounge, Aunt Irene by her side, as they watched the downpour.

'It can certainly rain here,' Irene Mortlake said.

Silently they watched the rain beat into the earth like an angry fiend, making the muddy water spurt up in all directions, digging deep

118

holes in the wet earth, forming channels that widened and deepened as the water swirled madly downhill.

Oddly enough, Charon and Aunt Irene were alone for once. Eleanor had hurried to her car to drive and fetch Jeremy and Keith who were at a Christmas party, Pippa and Robin had come running from the stables, drenched and laughing, and were having showers. Midge was having an unusual afternoon sleep after a series of Christmas parties, for once her energy seemed deflated.

'Charon, have you thought about your future?' Irene Mortlake's voice and words startled Charon.

'My future . . .?' Charon turned her head to took at the woman by her side. 'No . . . well . . .'

Irene Mortlake's face was grave. 'Charon dear, you're nineteen and you're never going to have to feel alone again. You know that. But life is just beginning for you. Have you thought about a career?'

'Well, I teach in nursery school . . .' Charon began and her face clouded. 'But only as an assistant. I wasn't about to take the full course . . .'

'D'you enjoy the work?'

Charon frowned thoughtfully. 'Yes, in a way but . . . well, you're always under someone and you have to do things her way and . . .'

'They're not always the way you'd do

things?'

Charon laughed. 'No.'

Irene Mortlake fidgeted uneasily. 'I was just thinking, Charon, that . . . well, I know Eleanor hopes that you'll stay here and live with them . . .'

'Always?' Charon was startled. Somehow her mind, forced to accept so much, had not faced up to the future.

'Yes, always. That is, of course, till you marry. I just wanted to say, Charon, that . . . that if you decide not to live here—and quite frankly, I find it rather a . . . a stagnant place to live though it is beautiful and everyone very friendly but . . . I don't think it's really a place for young people. You've lived such an insular secure sort of life . . .'

Secure! Charon forced herself not to smile. Hadn't Aunt Irene any idea of the insecurity felt by an orphan? Of course she meant the security of the Convent walls but that wasn't a real security, not like the security of being loved.

'Anyhow,' Irene Mortlake looked as uncomfortable as she felt. 'I don't want you to think I'm trying to persuade you any way, or that I'd do anything to upset Eleanor, but I just want to say, Charon, that if you *don't* want to stay here, you'll always be welcome in my home.'

'Why, that's awfully nice . . .' Charon began. 'You mean to stay . . .'

Irene flushed. 'No, I mean to live. Forever. I mean, till you get married or . . . or something. I'm not being kind or nice but purely selfish, Charon. I've always wanted a daughter and with Robin at the university my days are long and empty. We could have such fun, Charon. Drive all over Africa, later go overseas. I'm not being kind . . .'

'It sounds marvellous,' Charon said. And it was the truth, she knew it. Life with Aunt Irene would be uncomplicated, she wouldn't constantly probe into the past as 'Ma' did. But . . .

'There's no hurry, Charon. Don't rush into anything,' Aunt Irene continued. 'Just think about it . . . Ah, here they come . . .'

They watched Eleanor drive up from the gate, the car already slithering in the wet mud, the children shouting excitedly as they rushed into the house.

Eleanor came in. 'Bit chilly,' she said. 'It always gets cold up here when it rains . . .'

She lit the log fire and it soon crackled invitingly.

'Quite a few inches we're going to have,' she said and smiled at the others. 'You know Adam, Irene? The nice young doctor?'

Charon instinctively tensed, as Irene Mortlake nodded.

'Well, I met his mother. You really must come with me up there. She's a honey though the husband is a bit difficult at times but an excellent doctor. Well, Mrs. Bray was telling me that poor Adam is being deluged with letters and phone calls from his girl friend in Durban. He hasn't time to answer them but she can't seem to understand and rings up and talks to his mother . . .'

Charon slipped out of the room. Her limbs felt heavy and stiff and for the first time for ages, she felt depressed. In her own room, she scolded herself. What right had she to feel like this? Adam was a man of . . . well, about thirty, surely. Wouldn't it be rather odd if he didn't have a girl friend? And she must obviously love him a lot to chase him like that . . .

She heard the phone bell ring and Pippa shouting. As Charon went outside into the corridor, she bumped into an angry, red-faced Pippa.

'That girl again . . .' Pippa said crossly.

'That girl?'

'You know, the medical student that came here on Christmas day? She's making a play for Robin . . .' Pippa said.

'Is she?' Charon was startled.

'She's always ringing up. Now she's asked Robin to her party tonight and she hasn't asked any of us . . .'

'Perhaps she thinks you're . . .'

'Too young? Oh, I guess so but what about you? She could have had the decency to ask you . . .'

'I don't mind, Pippa,' Charon told her at

once. 'Honestly I don't. I'm really not the party-type . . .'

'D'you think he's in love with her?'

Charon shrugged. 'She was very pretty, I thought, and . . .'

'Robin's a man, I know. If only she'd leave him alone, though. I mean we won't have him much longer, will we . . . He'll be going back to Durban and university and . . .'

'He'll come up in the hols . . .'

'But it'll never be quite the same again, Charon. You can't think how wonderful it is to have a big brother . . .'

Can't I? Charon thought wryly how few people seemed to realise how much having a 'big' brother meant to her yet since they came up here, how little she'd seen of him. It was her own fault, of course, because she didn't mix properly and Robin was awfully good at trying to include her with them all the time. It wasn't his fault. It was her own.

She went back into her room and stood by the window. It was hard to see out for the rain was hitting the window viciously and everything was grey.

The future! That day she had been forced to think about her future seriously.

What did she want to do? Where did she want to go? With whom did she want to live?

These were all questions she had to answer. But how, she asked herself again and again.

For a moment, she wished she was back at

the Convent. Being governed by hostel rules, nursery school routine, the quiet but impersonal affection of the Nuns she'd known so long. At least, there, she'd never had to make a decision, never had any choice.

CHAPTER TWELVE

It rained for five days. By then, Adam was not only tired but tense with suppressed anger. He drove the old red car carefully over the muddy roads, skidding and slipping, perilously near the mountain drops, going from house to house as more calls came in. There was an epidemic of whooping cough, a mild one, but every parent whose child seemed to have a slight cough, sent out an S.O.S.

At the hospital there was chaos. Several unexpected cases of pneumonia amongst the older generation, a lot of bronchitis amongst the younger ones and the nurses and the three doctors in turn went down with 'flu.

In addition, Adam's father was steadily getting worse and just as steadily insisting that he was perfectly well and he didn't want 'a fuss' made! Added to which was the annoyance of Marie Fox.

Why couldn't she understand that he was busy, Adam wondered, as, stiff with tiredness, he drove the cranky old car towards his home.

He'd written and explained but apparently that wasn't enough. She was always 'phoning him and the calls would come through at the most inconvenient moments so, in the end, he'd had to arrange with the hospital exchange that her calls were to be put through to his home. His mother coped but she seemed to find it a great joke. He couldn't see anything funny in it at all. Why didn't the girl get off his back, he kept asking himself. Heaven knows he hadn't given her much encouragement.

The car coughed petulantly, coughed again and stopped. He managed to pull off the road on to the grass verge. He turned up his collar, pulled his hat down over his eyes and ventured out into the torrential rain, opening the car's bonnet, trying everything he knew, but still the engine refused to start.

It was the final straw and as he sat in the car, door half-open, while he watched for a passing car to give him a lift, he made up his mind.

Next week when the worst of the whooping cough should be over, he was going to fly down to Durban. First to collect his own car, which would be much easier to drive and infinitely more reliable, and secondly, to settle things with Marie Fox, no matter how unpleasant it should turn out to be!

He got the lift. He was surprised to recognise Leila Lawson for he'd heard that her husband refused to let her drive. Perhaps she noticed he was surprised for she laughed.

'Oh, Henry's in bed with 'flu,' she said. 'So he's got no choice but I do wish he'd choose nice summer weather to be *hors de combat* as I loathe, simply loathe, driving in the rain.'

'I don't blame you,' Adam agreed. 'How are the kids?'

She went red. 'Fine. Thanks to you and that nice girl.'

'Nice girl? Oh, you mean Charon Webb?'

'Who else? I went and saw her and thanked her because on that night I was a bit upset. She was very sweet and has offered to act as baby sitter when we want to go out. We're awfully pleased for Henry fetches her and drives her back and the kids adore her. Oh, we have a dog, you know. An Alsatian, so she's quite safe,' Leila added hastily.

Adam nodded but he found himself wondering how Charon felt about it, knowing, as he did, her fear of dogs.

Leila refused his invitation to go in for a drink or cup of coffee. 'No thanks, Henry's on edge while I'm out so I'd better get back.'

Adam went into the house, shook his macintosh on the covered-in stoep, and his hat, hung them up over chairs to drip and went in search of his father, first 'phoning the garage to ask them to tow the car to be repaired and to rent him one as from now.

'I may be sent for by the hospital at any moment,' he said curtly, 'so I'd be pleased if you could send one right out at once.'

He found his father huddled in his rocking chair near a log fire.

'The car packed up,' Adam said curtly, going to warm his hands.

'Never packed up when I was driving it . . .' the thin frail-looking old man said testily.

'That I don't believe . . .' Adam said, going to the sideboard and pouring two strong drinks. He was in a bad temper but, fortunately knew it and so could keep it under control.

He gave his father one glass and swallowed his strong Scotch.

'Next week, if the whooping cough is better, I'm flying to Durban . . .'

His father looked up, startled. 'Durban?' There was a sudden fear in his eyes. 'What on earth for?'

'Pick up my car.' Adam walked to the window. It was still raining but the forecast had been more cheerful. 'Dad,' he said abruptly, hoping he'd chosen the right moment. 'I want you to come with me.'

He swung round in time to see the 'frightened rabbit' look on his father's face.

'What on earth for?'

'Good grief, Dad, do I have to spell everything out for you? You are the most pig-headed, obstinate, truculent, selfish, egotistical . . .' he paused, as much for breath as because he was running out of adjectives.

There was a faint smile on the old man's face. 'Save your breath, son, I get the message. I'm not going, I don't need . . .'

'It isn't what *you* need, Dad—it's what Mum and I need,' Adam said, coming to stand by him, towering above him, thinking with sudden dismay how very frail his father looked. 'We're worried sick and you know it. All the acting in the world won't stop us from thinking what we are thinking. And what you're thinking, too.' He paused. 'Aren't you?' Adam shouted.

His father passed his hand nervously over the few wisps of hair he still had and then down over his face.

'Maybe I am but . . .'

'Well, then let's face facts. You never were a coward. I know that. You're trying to protect us from the truth. What we fear is much worse, Dad. You'll come with me?'

His father drained his glass and passed it, empty, to Adam.

'Another, please, son. Yes, I'll come,' he said and sounded very weary.

Adam was elated when he told his mother the news. So was she.

'I'll come along, too, Adam, dear boy. It'll be good fun to see the shops and that'll leave you free to fix up things with your adoring Marie . . .' She chuckled.

'To hell with Marie . . .' Adam said crossly.

She looked grave for a moment. 'Adam, are you sure you, well . . .' she gave an absurdly girlish sound, like a giggle, 'didn't lead her up the garden path?'

'Mother . . .' Adam pretended to be shocked but then changed his voice and became grave. 'Honestly, Mum, I don't think so. I've never been so rude to nor snubbed any girl so often as I have done to Marie. I wonder she condescends to talk to me. She just can't seem to understand.'

'Maybe if you told her there was someone else?' his mother suggested.

He frowned. 'But there isn't.'

'Couldn't you pretend? Not actually lie but sort of hint? That this chasing you with everyone in the town laughing about it, is embarrassing?'

Adam scowled. 'They are? How do they know?'

'My dear Adam, in a town as small as this people talk. The Exchange girls go off into hysterics when they put Marie through to me. They even say something like: "Here she is again, Madam, never gives up, does she?" before they switch Marie through to me. Then at the hospital . . . don't tell me tongues haven't been buzzing there.'

He sighed. 'I know. It's maddening. Well, I'll tell her there isn't a hope, Mum. I'll dot my i's and cross my t's until I make sure she understands.'

'Will it break her heart? I mean, she isn't the kind of girl who'd commit suicide?' his

129

mother said anxiously.

Adam burst out laughing. 'That's the last thing she'd do. Don't worry, Mum. Marie loves only one person—and that's Marie Fox. She's got a hide as thick as a rhino's. It won't be pleasant but I'll make her face up to the truth. I am not and never will be in love with her.'

'What sort of girl will you marry, Adam?'

They were sitting round the fire late in the evening. Adam had been out to three calls in the hired car, two of them insignificant, one serious. Now he shivered as he warmed his hands, rubbing them together, wondering for a moment if his father was, as he was supposed to be, sound asleep, or was he lying there awake, dreading the journey to Durban and what it would reveal.

'I've never thought about it, Mum.'

'You will marry, dear?' She sounded anxious.

He smiled at her. 'Not just for the sake of marriage, Mum. If I meet the right one . . .'

'What do you mean by the right one, Adam?'

He frowned a little. 'I don't quite know. A girl who doesn't fuss. Doesn't mind if I'm late for dinner. A girl . . .' He paused and smiled at her. 'A girl like you . . .'

'Flatterer . . .' she scolded, laughing. 'You're asking for perfection.'

'Dad got it. Why shouldn't I?'

'I don't know that your Dad did get it,' his

130

mother looked thoughtful. 'In our early days, I wasn't too easy to live with . . .'

'I bet the old boy hasn't been too easy, either.'

She smiled. 'No. That's marriage. Compromise, adjust, accept, be grateful for . . .'

'Doesn't sound too attractive to me,' he told her, his eyes amused.

She stood up. 'Time you were in bed, Adam. One day you'll meet a girl and all these fine qualities you seek for will no longer matter. I just hope you meet the right kind of girl . . . a nice girl.'

He bent and kissed her. 'I don't doubt that but if I don't find a *nice* girl, you will let me know.'

'You can be sure I will,' she promised him.

'If only it would stop raining . . .' Adam said as they said goodnight.

It was as though his prayer had been heard and answered for when they awoke the grey clouds had gone, the rain had vanished and the sun, with all its heat, was beaming down on them. Equally miraculously, the whooping cough epidemic simmered down, the bronchitis cases lessened, the old folk with pneumonia began to smile cheerfully and say they felt better already.

On Tuesday, Adam and his parents flew down to Durban. Here they found it very hot and appallingly humid. After the fresh bracing

131

air of the mountainous Amanzi, Durban seemed stuffy and overcrowded.

Dr. Bray was taken into a clinic. His wife, trying to hide her anxiety, spent her time going from shop to shop, as if intoxicated by their wares, then to cinemas, going to sit by her husband in between his tests. Adam went to the Foxes flat, dreading yet welcoming the task ahead of him.

Part of the task could not be tackled. Marie was away. Her parents told him that some friends of hers from Johannesburg had suddenly turned up on a tour of the South, planning to drive down to Cape Town by way of the Garden Route. Marie had joined them.

'She'll be sorry to miss you,' Mrs. Fox said, looking at him oddly. Uneasily Adam wondered just what Mrs. Fox had been told by Marie.

Then Adam had a long talk with Gerald Fox. At first the older man was inclined to anger and recriminations, then he calmed down and tried to point out to Adam the 'folly of his ways', finally he accepted it and helped Adam iron out any difficulties. At last, Adam was a free man, free of the partnership, its obligations and promising future—as far as financial security was concerned—and he knew he was very glad.

'I'm not sacrificing anything for my father,' Adam told Gerald Fox, who fingered his small pointed beard impatiently. 'I discovered up there that that is the way I want to work.'

'I think you must be out of your mind. The opportunities you had here. Marie will be very upset.'

'She'll understand when I explain.'

Adam was a happier man by the time he'd packed all his belongings and had moved out of the Fox's flat, into the hotel with his mother. He told neither his mother nor his father what he had done. He knew it would upset them for they would be convinced he had made this 'great sacrifice' for them, and find it hard to believe he had done it of his own free will and to please himself and no one else. Better to tell them later when the anxious time of suspense was over and they knew just what was wrong with Dr. Bray.

The verdict when it came was infinitely better than Adam had dared hope. He and his mother danced round the doctor's surgery with glee. It wouldn't be easy, keeping the old doctor in bed for six whole months but the long complete rest and the effect of certain drugs meant that, at the end of it, he should be able to lead a normal life, retired, of course, but otherwise normal. Their fears were unjustified. Oh, how glad they were they'd persuaded the doctor to come to Durban.

Dr. Bray took a different view. He'd have died before admitting it but he had thought he was dying. Now he knew he was going to live but what sort of life would it be? Doing nothing all day long! Why, he'd die of sheer boredom.

Adam drove them home slowly. The weather perfect, dust already beginning to rise from the earth roads. The only uncheerful person was old Dr. Bray who never ceased to grumble and complain and snap everyone's head off.

'Bear with him, Adam dear,' his mother said as they dined alone. ' 'Tis a hard burden for him to bear.'

Adam looked at her. 'You're the one carrying the burden, Mum. All he has to do is lie in bed and read and . . .'

'Fume. Poor darling. He's always been so active, felt so needed. But now, he'll feel no one wants him.'

The phone bell rang. The hospital!

'Yes, I am back. Who . . . ? Of course. I'll go there right away. Yes, you did quite right to call me,' he said cheerfully and went back to the stoep where his mother was sitting in the cool of the evening.

'Big trouble?'

'I don't know. Think I'll run up and ask Dad a few things. It's the Lillington boy. Keith. Got a bad attack of asthma. Dad's talked about them quite often . . .'

She beamed. 'A good idea, darling, then he won't feel so out of things . . .'

He had a quick talk with his father who wasn't very forthcoming and then Adam drove

134

up to the Lillington's house. They were all there, except Adam noticed, Robin.

'It came on without any warning, Adam,' Eleanor said worriedly.

'These attacks often do,' he said comfortingly.

They were sitting round the pool on the patio, great flaring torches sizzling with the mosquitoes they attracted. Vaguely he saw Charon smiling at him and he smiled back.

'By the way,' Sam said in his slow deep voice. 'How's the old doctor?'

'Fine . . .' Adam turned eagerly. 'We're so relieved. He's mad as can be, of course, for it means six months in bed and retirement.'

'Retirement?' Sam sounded shocked. 'That's bad news. What'll we do without him?'

Adam hesitated, tempted to tell them he planned to take over old Dr. Bray's practice, then he decided against saying anything. Even if they promised not to mention it, it was so easy to forget and once let the news get around . . . why, everyone would know it. This wasn't the right time to tell the old boy.

'You'll manage,' he said, cheerfully.

'Charon dear,' Eleanor said. 'I wonder if you would take Adam to see Keith. The boy seems happier when you're there . . .'

'Of course.' Charon stood up and led the way.

She was wearing a short, loosely-fitting green frock. Adam thought she looked unhappy and worried as they went into the brightly-lit house but put it down to anxiety about Keith.

The small boy was having a battle, Adam saw. He got to work at once and with Charon's silent but efficient help made sure that Keith was soon breathing with greater ease.

Adam stood up, looking down at the quiet boy, so different from the one who had joked and made absurdly wise comments at the Christmas dinner party. Keith's eyes were closed, but tightly shut, as if he was fighting the desire to open them. His hands too were tightly clenched, and his legs stiff.

Adam led the way outside. 'What started it off?' he asked as he made out the prescription.

Charon seemed to hesitate. 'It sounds conceited but . . .'

Adam looked up. 'But . . .?' he echoed impatiently.

'Well, Robin and Aunt Irene have to go back to Durban soon and I may be going with them . . .'

'You leaving here? I gathered that Eleanor wants you to stay . . .' He was startled.

'I gather she does but she hasn't said so. Not in so many words. Sam has. And . . . well, and Keith and Midge but . . .'

Adam sighed. 'Things are no better? You still haven't forgiven her?'

Charon raised her hands to her face. 'Please, Adam . . . don't. I've been over it again

136

and again and I am very very fond of Ma
but . . .'

'There's still the but . . .'

'Besides, it isn't only that . . .' Charon
lowered her hands and gazed at him. 'You see,
Ma has all these kids but Aunt Irene hasn't
anyone . . . only Robin and he's away at
University and . . .'

'You feel she needs you more?' Adam said.
'I suppose in a way, she does. But Charon, I
think it might be a good idea to stay on here
for a while. At least until Keith is back at
school with his days full—then you could talk
of going again and see the reaction. How
about that for an idea?'

He was startled by the delight on her face.
'Oh, thank you, Adam. That's the perfect
solution. This way, no one will get hurt.'

CHAPTER THIRTEEN

Grateful for Adam's advice, Charon told Sam
she'd like to stay with them but not for always
. . . She saw the hurt puzzled look in his eyes
and hastened to explain.

'Sam . . .' Somehow she had always been
able to call Sam Lillington that. 'It isn't that
I'm not happy here or that I don't like you all
terribly but . . .'

He nodded. He was stroking the head of

one of the children's horses. He'd taken Charon for a walk through the citrus orchards, kept the conversation going and then discreetly led her to the paddock. He was slightly disturbed by the girl's fear of animals—which he recognised, although she thought she had hidden it successfully—and wanted her to grow accustomed to them gradually.

'Well, Candy . . .' he spoke to the horse. 'We'll all miss Charon when she goes but I'm glad you're staying for awhile.' He smiled at her. 'It's sort of nice having you around.'

She flushed. 'That's very . . .' She bit her lower lip as it trembled. 'I feel so bad about it, Sam. You're all so wonderful to me and I . . .'

His warm hand closed over her bare arm. 'Now, Charon, stop blaming yourself. You're as bad as your mother in that respect. We all make mistakes, take the wrong decisions but are we supposed to walk through life ever after, carrying a burden of guilt? I don't think so. We can only do the best we can . . .'

He put her hand gently on the animal's forehead and without realising it Charon stroked the horse's skin.

She looked up in surprise as she realised what she was doing. The horse kept his head still as if in understanding.

'All the same, Sam . . .' Charon's voice thickened.

The short stoutish man's tanned face went

slightly red.

'Stop worrying about it, Charon. Time is the great healer and we've all the time in the world to wait. The trouble was you shouldn't have been told everything in one go. Robin meant well, bless the lad, but it must have been a terrible blow . . .'

'Blow . . . ?' Charon was startled.

But Sam nodded. 'Blow to discover so many people—people you'd trusted—had lied to you. All in good will, I'm not denying it, but all the same your whole life had been a lie. The Webbs would have been kinder to have told you from the start but they believed you could take the shock easier as you grew older. I reckon that's wrong. Now Irene did right in telling Robin, that's why he's so mature and well-balanced . . .'

'And I'm immature and not well-balanced?' Charon asked.

He smiled. 'Look, Charon, you've had two bad shocks. Let's face it, only time will heal the scars. Now you stay with us as long as you like then go and stay with Irene—she'll love having you—then come back to us any time you wish. There'll always be a welcome.'

'I feel Aunt Irene needs me more . . .' Charon hesitated but Sam gave her a strange look.

'That's where you're wrong, lass,' he said. 'Your real mother needs you more but only when you've forgiven her.'

'I'm sorry . . .' She bit her lip again and Sam took her hand and, swinging it gently, walked with her back to the house.

'Don't worry, Charon. It'll all work out. You'll see,' he said comfortingly.

But if Charon could talk to Sam and to 'Aunt Irene' who immediately accepted the fact that Charon wanted to stay a little longer, Charon couldn't tell her real mother. She tried a dozen times but how did you say:

'I'd like to stay a while because Keith needs me but then I'd like to go to Aunt Irene's . . .'

It sounded both abominably conceited and also selfish. Having nothing to do with 'Ma's' wishes, just taking it for granted that Ma would agree willingly no matter how she felt.

Her mother no longer kept asking probing questions about life in the Orphanage but a wall seemed to have grown up between them. A wall they had made together. Charon realised that just as she avoided being alone with her mother, so did Eleanor avoid being alone with her daughter. On the surface, all was well. Charon chatted to 'Ma' when the others were there but if she saw her in a room alone, Charon would quietly slip away. It was as though there was nothing more to be said— because if they spoke to one another they could only misunderstand and perhaps hurt one another.

Keith's asthma began to improve but he pretended to be asleep except when Charon sat with him. The books for lip reading and sign talking had come and they spent a lot of time studying it and learning to talk with their hands.

Then one day, Charon was alone on the stoep. There'd been a heavy shower of rain which had driven her in from the stoep; Sam Lillington was out on the lands somewhere, Keith was asleep; so was Midge. Pippa had gone riding with Jeremy, her face flushed with annoyance because Robin had refused to join them. Aunt Irene was in town shopping and 'Ma' in the kitchen, talking to the cook-girl.

'Charon, I must talk to you . . .' Robin said, coming outside suddenly.

She laid down her book. 'Something wrong?' she said sympathetically, glad of the chance to see Robin alone for she seldom did these days. If he wasn't in town with his new girl friend, he was playing tennis or riding with Pippa.

He sprawled on the swing chair by her side. He looked flushed and hot and . . . Charon saw with surprise, unhappy.

'I'll say there is, Charon. I'm in love . . .'

She was startled. 'That student . . . ?'

'Yes, Tess. Tess Darnley. Gee, I didn't think it'd hurt like this, Charon. I've been in love before but . . .' He whistled softly, pulled a packet of cigarettes from his shirt pocket and lit one.

'Doesn't she love you? Is that why it hurts?'

He looked at her sideways. 'No, it most certainly isn't. The big trouble is that she loves me, too, and we haven't a hope . . .'

'Haven't a hope?' Charon repeated. She hated to see Robin looking so upset. Normally he was such a happy person.

'No. You see, I'm at Durban Uni. and she's at Cape Town. I'm going to be a lawyer, she a doctor. Actually she's just finished her second year and is very keen. We might be able to get a transfer but I doubt it . . .'

'You mean, you're thinking of getting married?'

He grimaced. 'Don't look so shocked, Charon. It is the usual thing when you fall in love, you know.'

'But Robin, you can't . . .' Charon sat up and stared at him in dismay. 'You know what you said to me about students marrying. That they shouldn't, they should wait . . .'

'I wasn't in love then . . .'

'No, but Robin . . . couldn't you just be engaged?'

'And live a thousand miles apart?'

'You could spend the hols together and write . . .'

'Good grief . . .' Robin exploded. 'It's obvious you've never been in love . . .'

Charon stared at him worriedly. 'But your career, Robin. And hers . . . And . . . and . . . remember what you said about dreading the responsibilities of marriage. Suppose you do

142

get a transfer and marry and Tess gets . . . suppose she has a baby? I know your Mum has plenty of money so it wouldn't be so bad but how's she going to feel . . . Students shouldn't marry. You said so. You said it wasn't fair to the children . . .' Charon told him forcefully and then she caught her breath with dismay.

She had heard, and recognised, the soft tap-tap of Ma's high heels on the polished floor of the hall. Now they had gone. How much had Ma heard? Oh no, Charon moaned silently. Was she always going to hurt her mother? How could she have spoken like that? Like a prig. What right had she to judge . . . ?

She sighed and looked at Robin. He was stubbing out a cigarette angrily.

'I'm sorry, Robin,' she said quickly. 'It's your life, yours and Tess's. Have you told your mother?'

'My real one or my adoptive one?' he asked. She was shocked for it was the first time she'd heard him be bitter.

'Aunt Irene, of course.'

'No. I haven't told anyone but you. I thought you'd understand but I don't think you've ever been in love . . .'

'No, I haven't,' Charon said slowly. Was it completely true, she wondered. She often found herself thinking of Adam, though they met rarely. But could that be called 'love', she asked herself.

'It's terrible,' Robin said dramatically.

'Wonderful and ghastly if ever the twain shall meet.'

'How'll Tess's parents react?'

'She says they won't care. That they've no interest in her at all, just so long as she keeps out of their hair.'

'That sounds awful . . .'

'It must be. She needs someone, strong, reliable, to lean on, Charon . . . Don't look at me like that . . .' he said, standing up suddenly.

'I'm sorry, Robin. I didn't mean to look at you like anything. I was just thinking how wonderful it must be to be loved by someone like you . . .'

He bent and dropped a light kiss on her forehead.

'Don't worry, Charon, it'll happen to you, one day. Wham . . . just like that and you'll wonder what's hit you . . .'

'What will you do?'

'Just talk it over. We've talked it over already a million times but . . . Well, maybe, we'll work out a solution . . .'

'Robin, women do marry Merchant Seamen, and Army men and . . . well, their marriages are happy ones. Couldn't you and Tess marry and meet in the hols . . .'

'Not on your life,' Robin said firmly, running his fingers through his thick dark hair. 'When I have a wife, the home is the place for her.'

'But if Tess is a doctor, she won't often be at

home . . .'

'I shan't let her be a G.P.—she can do research or something that lets her keep respectable hours.'

Charon tried not to smile. 'Does she know this?'

'No, I haven't told her yet. After all, she may never become a doctor. Lots of students change their minds, you know.'

'Will you?'

'Good grief, no. Now, keep it under your hat, Charon, there's a good girl.'

'Of course I will but . . . but Robin, you won't do anything in a hurry?'

He stood in the doorway and smiled. 'You mean, elope? Course not. I'm not that much of a cad. I want Mum to be there at the wedding, weeping bitterly. She'll love it . . .' He chuckled and vanished.

Charon sat very still until she heard the roaring of his car and knew he had gone into town to see Tess. Then she relaxed. The sun was out again and the flowers on the bushes seemed to be rejuvenated, lifting their heads, a mass of deep reds, blues and an occasional yellow. She hardly noticed the beauty of the green grass, the distant mountains, the blue sky, for she was thinking about Robin and love.

He'd been so sure of himself before. Now he said it hit you without warning—'wham!'.

If she was in love with Adam, nothing had

hit her 'wham'! It was just that she liked him, felt safe with him, at ease. But that wasn't necessarily 'love' for she felt like that with Robin, Sam and Aunt Irene.

Charon wondered what it would be like to be married to a man like Adam. In the first place, you'd have to accept the strongest rival in the world—his work. Being a doctor would always come first. She wondered if that was hard for a girl, deeply in love, to understand. What about Marie Fox, the girl who was always ringing Adam up before he went to Durban? Apparently she hadn't rung him up since so they must have come to some arrangement. Perhaps they had agreed not to announce their engagement until his father was well and Adam could return to Durban. Charon wondered what sort of girl this Marie Fox was. How much Adam loved her. How much she loved Adam.

She thought she heard Keith call so she jumped up and hurried inside. Passing 'Ma' on the way. They smiled and spoke casually but Charon wanted to fling her arms round the older woman and apologise when she saw that 'Ma's' eyes were red, as if she had been crying.

The next day was very hot. Even Pippa's energy was defeated. They all lay round the swimming pool and were startled when Eleanor came out to join them, her eyes excited.

'What d'you think,' she said eagerly. 'I've

just seen Adam's girl friend.'

Robin sat up. 'What's she like?'

'Lovely. Absolutely gorgeous, Robin. She's very small and dainty, like a doll. A blonde and very elegantly dressed . . . Everyone's staring at her.'

'Where is she?' Robin asked.

'How d'you know she's Adam's girl friend?' Pippa joined in.

Charon sat very still, hugging herself for she suddenly felt cold.

'Staying at the Wayfarers Inn. I was talking to Mrs. Green when she booked in. She said she'd have a shower and then go up to the hospital to see her fiancé . . .'

'I didn't know they were engaged . . .' Aunt Irene said.

Eleanor chuckled. 'I don't think he does. She hasn't got a ring and she seemed in a bit of a temper. I know she's Adam's girl friend, Pippa, because she signed the register, Marie Fox and Adam's mother had told me about her . . .'

Robin jumped up. 'Let's go and see her . . . fresh local talent always welcomed . . .' he joked, pulling Pippa to her feet. 'Come on, Charon . . .'

'I don't think so . . .' she began but Robin had hauled her to her feet, giving her a slight tap.

'Go and put on something, shorts or a dress, and I must just comb my hair . . .'

Pippa smiled disdainfully. 'Planning to slay her?'

'I don't need to plan,' Robin told her with a grin. 'I just think a little healthy jealousy might do Tess good.'

Reluctantly Charon slid out of her swimsuit and into a pair of cream culottes and a cream shirt. She brushed her hair and spent more time than usual on making-up her face so that Robin came to pound on her door impatiently.

'We don't want to miss her . . .'

The three of them crowded into the M.G. and he drove to town quickly, the warm wind blowing their hair about, Charon feeling more miserable with every moment. Wasn't this rather childish, rushing into town to look at a girl who might be Adam's girl friend? Wouldn't Adam think it bad manners? In any case, she thought miserably, she'd got no desire at all to see this beautiful, elegant, doll-like creature.

Robin parked the car, took the two girls by the arm, and led the way up the steps to the thatched stoep before the hotel. He looked handsome, Charon thought, glancing at him sideways, with his thick dark hair, and dark eyes. Now he looked a bit startled as he stared at two girls sitting at a table.

'Tess . . .' he said.

Charon saw Pippa's face stiffen, guessed how she felt for Pippa was at the age when you had a crush on someone and her newly found

148

stepbrother Robin was that someone.

Tess was lovely but in quite a different way from the dainty, doll-like girl by her side. Tess had a defiant air.

'Well, look who's here,' she said, her voice sarcastic. 'How fast news travels . . . Marie, meet Robin Mortlake . . . his sister, Charon Webb . . . oh, don't look so startled, it's all very involved and this is Pippa Lillington. Folks, needless to say, this is Marie Fox. Care to join us . . . ?'

Her eyes were flashing furiously as she looked at Robin, Charon saw, but she also saw the smile he gave Tess and the way the anger left her.

They sat down. 'You knew Marie Fox?' Robin sounded surprised.

'And why not? We went to school together.'

'Only you're from Cape Town and she's from Durban . . .'

'You seem to know a lot about me . . .' Marie Fox said, her voice cold and sharp as an icicle.

Charon stared at her. Fascinated and horrified. Could Adam be in love with this fantastic creature? Beautiful? Of course she was with perfect features, the right kind of nose, the perfectly arranged blonde hair, the lovely shocking-pink silk suit, slender lovely legs. She was perfect. Until you looked into her innocent blue eyes and saw they were as hard and cold as steel.

The waiter brought them cold drinks. Marie glanced at the gold watch on her wrist. 'I don't want to be too long. I phoned the hospital and they said Adam was out but should be back by twelve.'

'Is he expecting you?' Robin asked casually, offering cigarettes, getting up with an exaggerated bow of politeness as he lighted them for the girls.

Marie smiled. If a smile it could be called, Charon thought and then was ashamed of herself. How catty could you get, she wondered.

'No. He's getting the shock of his life,' Marie said smugly. 'Shock tactics, that's the way to handle men like Adam. I'm so mad at him I'll probably grab his surgeon's scalpel and cut his throat.'

'Mad at him?' Tess's eyes sparkled. 'Why, what's he done?'

'It's what he hasn't done that's made me mad. Comes down to Durban when I'm at the Cape and calmly breaks his partnership. The partnership I fought madly to get him. Anyone who's lucky enough to work with Dad has a secure future. But that . . . that . . . that idiot has thrown it all away . . .' she said, her voice vicious.

Charon, shocked, glanced at the others. Robin was looking amused, Tess, by his side, rather startled and Pippa, frankly puzzled.

The small, perfect but cold face of Marie

150

was like a mask, Charon thought, as the husky angry voice went on:

'But I know Adam, well. He's like all men with ideals and ridiculous ideas of ethics. He's clay in a clever woman's hands. That's why he's here—why he's thrown away the chance of a lifetime. The chance many young doctors would give anything to have. It's all his mother's fault. There's this gentle but weak streak in Adam. She's possessive and knows how to morally blackmail him. You see, it was all nonsense about the old doctor's illness. Just senility, that's all it was. But she got Adam up here . . .' She looked round at the silent faces.

'D'you know what we call Adam in Durban?' she asked, her voice silky. No one answered her but she went on: 'We call him the *Dutiful Doctor*, because he always does what his mother says . . .'

She jumped up. 'Sorry to have to leave you but I'll be seeing you?'

Pippa suddenly found her voice. 'I know Mum would like to meet you. Perhaps you and Adam would like to come up tonight? We're having a braaivleis and some friends in. Nothing formal. Just come about six for we have drinks, first.'

Marie's eyes flicked round at them all. 'Thanks. I'll ask Adam. It sounds terrific so I'm sure we'll be with you.'

She tripped—literally tripped like an imaginary fairy doll, Charon thought angrily—

down the steps to the long, low cream car. Got behind the wheel, lifted her hand in farewell, started the engine and roared off . . .

They waited until she had gone out through the gates, then Pippa said: 'I hope she knows about the cows and goats roaming along the roads. If she drives at that rate . . .'

'Oh, her head's screwed on all right . . .' Tess said, her voice bitter.

'I thought she was your friend,' Robin said.

Tess laughed. 'Some friend. I don't think. We all hated her. There's something evil about her . . .'

Charon shivered. Was Marie the girl Adam loved? Was Marie right when she called Adam 'weak' and 'easily led'? Would she 'handle' Adam as she'd said she could? Was Adam the type of man to let a girl rule his life? And how could she love him, and still talk to him in that scathing sarcastic way, Charon wondered unhappily.

Then she realised something else. According to Marie Fox, Adam had severed his partnership and planned to live in Ukoma, taking over his father's practice. That changed a lot of things in Charon's mind. One of the threads that drew her to living in Durban with Aunt Irene had been the knowledge that Adam would be there. But now he'd be up here . . . unless . . .

Unless Marie talked him out of it and took him back, like a repentant runaway school-boy to shelter under her father's wing.

'What did you think of her, Robin?' Charon asked.

He looked at her, his face grim. 'Adam must be out of his mind to have anything to do with her. One meets that type of girl occasionally. There's only one word for her and Pippa's too young for me to say . . .' He gave Pippa a warm smile, 'but it begins with b and ends with h.'

CHAPTER FOURTEEN

Adam looked at the chart and then at the baby. Then at the Sister by his side. He smiled approvingly.

'Good work . . .'

She flushed. 'Good surgery, Doctor.'

'The jockey can't win without the horse . . .' he said, his face solemn.

'The horse wouldn't try without the jockey,' she told him, her eyes twinkling.

One of the African orderlies came hurrying. There was a young lady to see the doctor. She had phoned earlier but refused to give her name and had been told he would be back at twelve o'clock.

'She is rather angry,' he added. 'We put her in your office, Doctor Bray.'

'To see me?' Adam frowned. Who on earth . . . then he wondered if it would be Charon.

But she wouldn't be 'rather angry'. He shrugged, gave the Sister some quick instructions and promised to be back as soon as he could get rid of this unwelcome visitor and strode down the highly polished corridor to his office. He glanced out of one of the windows. The sun was shining and a group of walking patients were sprawled on the grass under the two weeping willows. Most of them were men wearing enormous white night shirts that nearly reached the ground, their dark faces alight as they talked and joked. A few plump African women were crouched on the grass verge of the drive, piles of oranges and bananas before them that they sold to the African patients.

His hand on the handle of the door, he paused for a moment. Who the devil could be demanding to see him like this?

He pushed the door and stood, startled into stillness. The diminutive dainty figure by the window slowly turned round and then Marie moved lightly, almost running across the room to him, her arms out, her mouth lifted alluringly.

'Adam, darling Adam . . . at last. What a battle it was to see you . . .'

She clung to him tightly but he did not bend down and kiss her, as he might have done in the past. He was only aware of anger. Of white blinding anger and frustrated irritation. If Marie noticed his coldness and lack of return,

154

she ignored it, moved away, closed the door behind him and leaned against it so that, short of lifting her out of the way, he could not leave the room.

'Adam . . .' Her voice was soft and beguiling. 'Tell me it isn't true? Tell me Dad made a mistake . . . tell me . . .'

'Tell you what?' he said curtly.

'Tell me it's not true that you want to bury yourself in this . . . this dead-alive hole. Tell me it isn't true, Adam darling. I know your mother wants you to settle up here, I know she's tried every weapon in her power to persuade you but . . .' Her voice was rising, losing its husky allurement as her anger gained command. 'Adam, it isn't true, is it? You haven't broken up the partnership?'

'It is true,' he said quietly.

She was like a child in a tantrum, almost out of her mind, he thought and felt rather sorry for her. She brushed by him, going to the window, face as white as snow, as she clenched and unclenched her hands, while obviously trying to regain control of herself. She looked round her wildly and he sensed the turmoil inside her, the childish longing to hurt him, to destroy everything that belonged to him. He saw her eyes flicker over the pile of notes on his desk, the files on the table by the window, and then he saw she'd gained control.

'Adam,' her voice was quiet. 'We're sensible intelligent adults. We mustn't fight like this.

Isn't there somewhere we can go and talk quietly.'

'Not this morning. I'm much too busy . . .'

'Busy! In this dump? What is there to do . . .' she sneered.

'Plenty. Care to walk round the wards?' he asked, knowing perfectly well that it was the last thing in the world she'd want to do.

He took her arm and opened the door, leading her down the corridor, past the reception office, out into the blinding sun to where her cream car waited for her.

'I'll be free for an hour this afternoon,' he told her. 'If nothing crops up, that is. Where are you staying?'

'At the Wanderers' Arms. I knew your mother wouldn't invite me to your home. She can't bear the sight of me.'

'You're completely wrong there,' he said quietly. 'She finds you very beautiful.'

'How charming of her . . .' Marie said bitterly. 'Then I'll see you at the hotel about . . .'

'Three o'clock. I'll do my best to be punctual, Marie, but . . .'

'I know, I know . . .' she said wearily. 'Work always comes first. I'll be in all the afternoon. I'll sleep—nothing else to do in this god-forsaken hole—so come when you can . . .'

Adam stood still as the expensive cream car roared off. He hoped she'd drive more carefully than she usually did for the African children, like the cattle, were apt to wander over the roads.

He went back to the Children's Ward, a little uncomfortable, conscious of curious glances and—was it—suppressed amusement? How much of what Marie had said, had they heard, he wondered. Her voice had been shrill enough—the voice, his mother would have said, of a fish-wife!

And then he remembered something. Something important. He put a call through to the hotel but Marie wasn't there. He left a message, asking the receptionist to tell Miss Fox not to mention the matter of the partnership to anyone as no one else knew about it.

'It's rather urgent,' Adam said.

The man at the other end seemed to understand. 'Some women have big mouths, sir. I'll tell her . . .'

Adam glanced at his watch. Just twenty minutes past twelve. And still so much to do . . .

He was late home for lunch as an emergency operation had had to be done. A child injured in a car crash but fortunately whisked to the hospital in time to save her life. It was two o'clock by the time he got out of his car at home. As soon as he went inside the house, he felt tension.

His mother came hurrying, her eyes red. 'Dear, you shouldn't have done it . . . Not even for us. Your father is so upset . . .'

'Shouldn't have done what . . .?' he began but the coldness in his stomach told him the answer. That little . . .

'Adam . . .' his father roared. 'Come here at once . . .'

Feeling absurdly like a boy hauled up before his headmaster, Adam strode into the small study where his father sat by the window.

'Adam, you had no right to do that without telling us. We don't need your help . . . you had no right to sacrifice . . .' His voice that had begun angrily now trailed away miserably and Adam saw that it was all the old man could do not to cry.

'Dad—has that blasted . . .' He bit back the word he knew his mother hated. 'Has Marie Fox been here making trouble?'

Mrs. Bray dabbed her eyes. 'She was, well . . . rather unpleasant, dear. She accused us of moral blackmail, of being leeches, leaning on you, demanding your life . . . she said you had the chance of a lifetime in Durban and . . .'

Adam's mouth was a thin line. 'Did she know you didn't know?'

'I think she must have done, dear, because of the way she put it. She began by asking if we were satisfied with the results of our . . . what she kept calling "moral blackmail". She told us that she'd been away and that you'd given up the partnership without telling her and that you and she were engaged to be married

158

and . . .'

'That's the lie,' Adam said and saw the relief in his mother's eyes. 'Look, sorry I'm late but there was a last minute panic. How about strong drinks for us all and then I must eat before going down and coping with that little . . .'

'But Adam . . .' his father said, his face more gaunt than ever, his breathing fast. 'You mustn't make this sacrifice for us. It's your life, your future . . .'

Adam poured stiff drinks and made his mother sit down and then straddled a chair, looking at them all.

'First, let's get one thing clear. I am neither engaged to Marie Fox nor have I any desire or intention of marrying her. She's a stubborn, predatory unhealthy, little . . .' His mouth closed angrily and then he gulped down some more Scotch, feeling the warmth of it easing away some of his anger. 'In the second place, I am making no sacrifice.'

He put his glass down and leaned over the back of the chair, moving his hands as he talked, with their long supple fingers.

'Dad—I really believed that my way lay in the cities in the beginning. There, I felt, I'd get more experience. I've discovered I've been trapped into a prison I loathe. I didn't talk about it for I was the fool—I'd walked into it with my eyes open. I was just a stooge. Like the other young partners. We just stood by when needed, never having the chance to make a decision or do anything we wanted to. We were puppets—dancing to a tune. I had a good bit of voluntary hospital work which I liked so that made up for it all a bit but . . . Coming up here, taking over what I've always secretly seen as a "dead end", opened my eyes. Here I'm on my own, half the time. I get to know the patients, from beginning to end. They're people. No longer just strange names. I like working here. I get on well with Dhlamini as well as with Frost and Cupstan. I like it here. It seemed a chance in the million for me to buy your practice from you as you're retiring so . . . while in Durban, I saw Dr. Fox.'

'Why didn't you tell us?'

He smiled at them, stood up to refill his glass and his father's for his mother was still sipping hers.

'Look, we were all emotionally involved. Worried about Dad. Then Dad had the shock of enforced retirement to meet. It's a hard task for any man, even harder for one as active as you, Dad. I knew you'd worry about this, that you might find it difficult to believe I'm doing this for myself and not for you. But please believe me . . .'

He looked at them both and smiled ruefully. 'Maybe you'd prefer it if I played the part of the heroic martyr who gives up the chance of a lifetime because of his devotion to his beloved parents? But it wouldn't ring true, Dad, for

I'm not the type. I'm as ambitious about my future as you are for me. Once I get used to this place, I'll have more free time and can get to work on that book I want to write. I thought you might find time to do some research for me, Dad. I'd be grateful for that takes time . . .'

Gradually, very slowly, but eventually, he believed he had convinced them that he was telling the truth. He was pleased when his father showed some enthusiasm about the research he'd do, but by the time he'd eaten his lunch and had driven to the Wayfarers' Hotel, Adam's anger was rising again.

He stopped at the reception desk. There was a man there. Adam introduced himself. 'Were you able to pass on the message?'

The man nodded. 'Sure, Doctor. Miss Fox came in just as I downed the receiver and I gave her the message.'

Adam hesitated. 'What did she do?'

'Turned round and went out into her car again, zooming away. She got back for lunch, though, and is up in her room, now. She's got a suite, doctor . . . She's used to the very best, I gather . . .' He gave a wink and Adam laughed.

'Or what she calls the very best,' Adam said.

He went up the curving staircase slowly. Knocked on the door of No. 12 and when he heard a faraway voice, opened the door.

It was a sitting-room, quite pleasantly furnished with rather heavily antique furniture, a dark crimson rug and matching curtains. On the green-covered sofa, Marie lay. She had changed into long yellow trousers and a thin yellow silk blouse, her hair was spread out over a dark cushion. Now she waved a hand vaguely.

'Good Adam—only five minutes late . . .' she said gaily.

He got a chair and straddled it, facing her but some way away.

'Why did you go and tell my parents?' he said coldly.

She sat up and looked offended. 'Tell them? They knew . . .'

'They did not and you know it,' he said, his anger still under control. 'I phoned a message to you asking you . . .'

'What message? I didn't get a message,' she said, her eyes wide with innocence.

He sighed. 'Look, Marie, it's time you grew up. I checked that they gave you the message and you went straight out and saw my parents . . .'

She sat up, her eyes snapping. 'Why, you nasty . . . you snooped on me . . .'

'You lied. You went to my home and deliberately upset my parents . . .'

'Upset them. They're too tough to be upset. All they want is you . . .'

'Marie, listen to me.' His stern voice jerked her back to stillness. 'I've given up the partnership because I wanted to. It's not for them. It's for me. I felt stifled down there, I

162

never had a chance to practise medicine. I just did what your father and his friends told me to do. I prefer this sort of life . . .'

She stood up very slowly. He wondered how often she had practised it before a mirror. Quite a number of times, he thought with a wry amusement, for she did it perfectly.

'You mean, you *want* this kind of a life?' She sounded shocked, wounded, and very hurt.

'Yes, I want this kind of life.'

She came to stand in front of him, legs slightly apart, hands on her hips as she looked down at him.

'Then you must choose between me and this way of living. I'd die up here after two days.'

'I have already chosen,' he said coldly.

She stared at him. 'You're prepared to lose me?'

He looked up. 'How can I lose you when you were never mine?'

'But I was . . . I love you. I thought we were going to be married. That's why I got you in with Dad . . . I knew you'd said nothing to me because you're one of those stupid ethical fools who feel too poor to ask a rich girl to marry him. I got you that partnership . . . I got you everything and . . .'

Adam stood up and then felt uncomfortable for he seemed to be towering threateningly over Marie so he hastily sat down again, he preferred staring up at her angry face.

'Marie,' he said slowly. 'Stop acting like a

spoilt child and face facts. Never at any time have I said I love you. Never have I mentioned marriage . . .'

'You kissed me . . .'

He smiled. 'Twice. If you call those pecks kisses. You lifted your face, obviously expecting a kiss and how could I refuse you? You'd have been hurt and furious with me. Look, Marie, let's treat this sensibly. You and I don't fit. You're socially-minded. You'll be a wonderful wife for a diplomat, a V.I.P. or even any ambitious man. Not for me, though. As my wife, you'd be lonely, bored to tears and utterly frustrated for I'd never come up to the standard you expect. Look, I don't love you and if you were honest, you'd admit that you don't really love me.'

'I never have loved you . . . you stupid conceited . . .' She almost spat the words at him.

He stood up, put the chair back where he'd found it, and looked at her. 'Good. That settles that. Kindly keep out of my hair in future, Marie, that's all I ask . . .'

His hand was on the door when she caught hold of his sleeve. She gazed up at him imploringly, her eyes wide so that if he hadn't really known her, he felt sure he'd have felt sorry for her.

'You'll take me to the Lillington's party tonight.'

He made a grimace of distaste. 'No . . .'

'Please . . . please . . . Adam,' she pleaded. 'Don't make me lose face. Then I'll walk out of your life and you'll never see me again.'

'All right,' he said reluctantly. 'I'll pick you up at six o'clock. You're sure they asked me?'

'Quite sure. I couldn't possibly go alone . . .' she said, her voice wistful.

Gently he detached her fingers from his sleeve and escaped. He ran down the stairs as though a fiend was on his heels and saw the amused glance the man behind the reception window gave him. How many people, Adam wondered, at this moment were talking about the 'young Doctor' and his girl friend!

CHAPTER FIFTEEN

The Lillingtons were fond of giving braaivleis parties to their friends, Sam enjoying himself at the gridiron as he fried steaks and sausages, everyone loving the quiet relaxed atmosphere as they sat around, on chairs or on the grass. This night was no exception, there was a quiet hum of conversation with a sudden laugh and every now and then drinks were passed round and small savouries.

It was one of those perfect summer evenings you get in South Africa, which are hard to forget with the magic of a black sky spangled with shining stars and, in this case, with a young crescent moon riding above the huge dark mountains, but every now and then being hidden as a small cloud drifted across it. The frogs were croaking loudly, giving warning of rain to come, but no one took any notice for the night was pleasantly warm without being too hot.

Charon helped Eleanor pass round the savouries, Aunt Irene and Robin looked after the drinks, and Charon thought what a really pleasant atmosphere it was. Yet all the time, she knew she was waiting . . .

Waiting for Adam to come—with Marie Fox.

Charon had asked Pippa why she'd asked them. Pippa had chuckled. 'I thought Mum would get a kick out of it. She's longing to know the sort of girl Adam likes and this'll give her something to talk about over coffee for months.'

It was true. 'Ma' had an insatiable interest in people, she loved to work out what made them 'tick', and undoubtedly Marie was an interesting specimen to study!

'All the same,' Pippa had gone on, 'I hadn't realised just how nasty Marie could be. Now I wish I hadn't asked them. Her tongue, I guess, is tipped with acid. Funny, Chary, you wouldn't think such a beautiful girl with everything in life she wants would have to be so downright nasty.'

Everything but Adam, Charon thought, or

166

was Marie right, and did she know how to handle men? Was she handling Adam right now, persuading him to change his mind?

Now as she moved around, talking to the guests, helping out when she saw something to do, Charon felt a strange anger growing inside her, a new indignation. It was not like her to hate anyone so much, yet how could she help hating Marie when she pretended to love Adam, yet could speak so scathingly about him? 'Dutiful Doctor,' she had called him, sneering because he was a good son. Was that a crime? Charon had read somewhere that a good son makes a good husband. Somehow, though, she couldn't see Adam as Marie's husband. Nor, for that matter, Marie as a doctor's wife.

There was a sudden stir and everyone seemed to turn his, or her head. Marie Fox stood on top of the stairs leading down to the patio and lawn. She stood dramatically, obviously enjoying the sensation she caused, the vivid glare of the blazing torches, set up at intervals, making her trouser suit of blue and silver sparkle, her blonde hair was brushed up into an elaborate hair-do and sparkled with diamanté-trimmed combs. Then Adam stepped forward, his tall thin body towering above the fragile-looking, dainty, doll-like beauty.

Something like a long sigh broke the stillness and then everyone was talking and laughing again. Someone produced a chair for Marie, someone else a drink, a group stood round as Adam introduced her. Charon, moving around, noticed the way the men hovered round Marie, rather, Charon thought with quick amusement, like bees round a plant noted for its pollen!

But gradually the group seemed to dissolve. Adam had vanished and Charon noticed that now Marie was moving round the different guests, sitting for a moment near one, talking to her, before moving on. She laughed gaily but her voice always dropped when she was talking. Charon was rather puzzled. It didn't seem in keeping with Marie's character, somehow. Charon would have expected Marie to sit on her chair as if it was a throne and wait for people to come to her.

Then Charon caught a word as she passed close to Marie.

'. . . the wisest thing to do under the circumstances . . .' Marie was saying sadly.

Later, Charon heard Marie say, 'Yes, we were very upset but . . . *c'est la vie* . . .'

Charon got herself a plate of sausages and a roll and butter and quietly sat down behind Marie, certain Marie wouldn't have noticed her in the semi-darkness. Charon saw that Marie was talking quietly to Mrs. Eaton. Charon immediately recognised her as one of the biggest gossips in town, according to 'Ma'. Charon pretended to eat and edged herself nearer and nearer, keeping behind them, hoping no one would notice that she was doing that despicable thing: eavesdropping!

What she heard, shocked her terribly. She sat very still, frozen with anger, as she heard Marie's wistful voice, telling lies, implying unspeakable things. Poisonous dangerous lies, for people were quick to pass them on and eager to say 'There can't be smoke without fire . . .'

'Yes, I was terribly hurt . . .' Marie was saying. 'I loved Adam so much but there are limits . . . Dad's a tolerant man but even he had to admit it was best for Adam to leave quietly now rather than wait until it all blew up . . .'

The torches flickered and Charon could see the hungry, excited look on Mrs. Eaton's lined thin face.

'How terrible for you, my dear, but what did he actually *do*?'

'I couldn't tell you . . .' Marie said with a very realistic break in her voice. 'I can't bear to talk about it. I only know I could never trust him again . . .'

Suddenly it was more than Charon could bear. She scrambled to her feet, spilling her sausages down her thin white frock, stumbling round Marie's chair and facing her.

'You've got to tell us what he did . . .' Charon said, her voice louder than she realised. 'You can't sit there and lie like that,

Marie Fox . . .' Charon was so angry she could feel her body trembling and her voice was unsteady.

Marie blinked up at her, looking startled. 'I don't understand . . . Are you drunk?'

'You understand only too well, Marie Fox,' Charon said, her voice rising. 'I've heard the lies you've been telling everyone. You're trying to make them distrust Adam . . .'

Charon suddenly realised that there was no sound but her voice. She looked round and everyone was staring at her as if she was mad.

With an involuntary movement, Charon held out her hands appealingly. 'I don't know how many of you have heard the lies Marie Fox has been saying about Adam tonight but I can tell you it's not true. Adam left Durban of his own will—he has never ever done anything to be ashamed of . . . at the St. Christopher's Clinic, the Sisters thought highly of him . . . far more than they thought of your father . . .' Charon said to Marie who sat, looking stunned. 'Who only thinks of money . . .'

Marie Fox's voice was cool and silvery: 'Are you out of your mind? Accusing me of telling lies . . . ?'

'Then if you're not telling us lies, tell us what Adam has done . . .' Charon said angrily. 'It's so easy to hint at things. If you're telling the truth, tell us what Adam did . . . If you don't tell us, we'll know you're lying . . .' Charon looked round at the silent shocked faces. 'Won't we . . . ?'

Mrs. Eaton answered. The only voice in the quietness.

'I agree, Miss Fox. I think you must tell us . . . You said it was something too terrible to talk about . . .'

Marie stood up, looked scathingly at Mrs. Eaton. 'Is this a conspiracy? I said nothing of the sort . . .'

'You did,' Charon said, 'for I heard you. So it was all lies?'

Marie looked up at Charon and smiled. 'All right—I'll tell them. Adam led me to believe that we were to be married soon and now he's let me down. He's not a good man nor a good doctor . . .'

Charon's hand flew out and hit Marie's left cheek. Charon caught her breath in horror. She hadn't meant to hit Marie . . . her hand had moved of its own accord. Now as she heard the startled shocked exclamations from the people around her, saw the red marks of her fingers on Marie's face, Charon, her eyes blinded with tears, turned and stumbled away . . .

Then Sam was there. 'Come with me, Charon . . .' he said, and then his voice changed. 'Robin will take you back to the hotel, Miss Fox . . .'

'She hit me . . .' Marie's voice rose hysterically. 'You all saw that. She hit me . . .'

From far away, Charon heard Robin speak.

'Pipe down. You asked for it,' he said curtly. 'We happen to be friends of Adam . . .'

And then Charon was stumbling up the steps, glad of Sam's hand under her elbow helping her. In the lounge, she wept and he got her a drink and made her sit down.

'I'm so sorry, Sam . . .' Charon sobbed. 'But she was telling wicked lies about Adam . . .'

Sam took her face in his hands gently and kissed her.

'Don't apologise, Chary, we're proud of you. Thank god you did hear what she was saying . . .'

Adam stood in the doorway. 'Something wrong?' he asked.

Sam glanced up. 'Where have you been?'

'Playing chess with Keith. I didn't feel in a party-mood.'

Sam gave an odd smile. 'That girl friend of yours has been spreading rumours about you and Charon slapped her face . . .'

Adam looked startled. 'Marie? I might have known it. She begged me to bring her here to "save her face" . . .'

'And instead she tried to slit your throat . . .' Sam said dryly. 'Thanks be, Charon overheard her talking and nipped it in the bud . . .'

'Thanks, Charon . . .' Adam came to stand near her. 'Why are you crying?'

Charon dabbed her eyes. 'Because I shouldn't have lost my temper . . . I mean, you shouldn't smack anyone in the face and scream at them . . .'

'You used Marie's language,' Adam said dryly. 'Probably the only language she understands. I'd better go and collect her and take her back where she belongs.'

'Robin's done that,' Sam said, standing up. 'Keep an eye on Charon for me, Adam. It's rocked her quite a bit . . . then come and join us. Plenty of food . . .' Sam looked down at Charon. 'I'm proud of you, child. Only wish I had a friend as eager to leap to my defence as Adam has . . .' He left them.

Adam sat down, offered Charon a cigarette. She rarely smoked but now she accepted a cigarette and tried to stop trembling. Never in her whole life had she been so angry before. Nor had she ever behaved so badly, before, she reminded herself. Sam had been kind to her but he must be feeling ashamed of the way she'd acted. She'd spoiled the party . . .

'Now tell me, Charon, what did she say about me?' Adam asked casually.

She looked at him unhappily, twisting her hands together.

'I didn't hear all of it, of course. I noticed she was moving around quite a bit talking to different people and when I passed near her, I'd hear her saying something like "I was terribly upset" or "It was terrible to hear . . ." and then when she deliberately sat down next to Mrs. Eaton, I got really worried.'

Adam gave a little laugh. 'The local gossip.'

'Yes, but that isn't all. Ma said once that Mrs. Eaton always adds bits to her gossip so that in the end, they're quite completely different from the truth. I sat behind Marie where I could listen . . . I know I shouldn't have but . . .' She stared at him but he merely nodded so she went on: 'Then I heard her implying that her father had asked you to leave Durban before you were exposed or something . . . she said it broke her heart but some things you couldn't accept and . . . It wasn't so much what she said, Adam, but the way she said it, implying the most terrible things. Mrs. Eaton wanted to know what you had done and Marie said it was too awful to talk about . . .' Charon paused to get her breath back.

'That . . . that was when I lost my temper. I got up, rushed round to face her and accused her of lying. I asked her to tell us what you had done and when she refused I said she was lying because there was nothing to tell . . . Then . . . then she said you'd promised to marry her and had let her down . . . that you were a bad doctor and a bad man and I . . .'

Adam looked as if he was trying not to smile. 'I slapped her face,' she went on.

He stared at her thoughtfully. 'I wonder what Mother Superior would have to say to that.'

Charon's face went bright red. 'She'd have been horrified. She said we must never lose our tempers, our self-control or dignity . . .'

174

'And I'm sure she would have said Marie should turn the other cheek . . .' Adam said dryly. 'What happened next?'

'Well, I realised how terribly I'd behaved and Sam rescued me . . . I'm sorry, Adam.'

He frowned. 'Sorry? What for?'

'Well, behaving like that . . .'

He stood up and came to sit by her side, taking her hand in his, gently flexing her fingers.

'I'm the one who should apologise, being weak enough to bring that little vixen here. I should have known she wanted her revenge . . .'

'Adam, she'll lie about you in Durban . . .'

He smiled. 'Don't worry about it, Charon. People who know Marie won't believe her. People who don't know her, will soon realise that she lies all the time . . .'

'I thought you were in love with her?'

Adam let out a loud laugh. 'Not on your life. That girl's been on my back since the day I met her. Tell you something, Charon, I don't know why but she seems to have made up her mind there and then to marry me. What I want or the small unimportant part of loving one another, seems to have no place in her scheme of things. She's been chasing me and I've told her a hundred times I am not in love with her nor do I want to marry her . . .'

'There's something nasty about her,' Charon said and shivered. 'Like a slug.'

Adam smiled. 'You could be right. She definitely isn't well-balanced. Personally I think she's had everything in life too easily and it makes her mad when she can't get what she wants . . .'

Someone came into the room. Adam and Charon looked up. It was Irene Mortlake.

'All right, Charon?' she asked cheerfully. 'Aren't you and Adam coming out?'

Charon gave an odd little smile. 'I feel ashamed. I shouldn't have lost my temper like that. I'm sure everyone was shocked . . .'

Aunt Irene bent down and kissed her. 'On the contrary, everyone admires you. I only wish I'd been near enough to slap her. Horrible creature . . .' She looked at Adam. 'Sorry if I offend you but she's a nasty bit of work.'

Adam laughed and stood up, gently dropping Charon's hand. 'And that's no lie,' he said with a laugh. 'Ever since the day I met her, I've been running like a frightened rabbit. Come on, Charon, my little defender . . .' he spoke jokingly but when Charon looked up at him, she saw a strange, new expression in his eyes. Almost as if he was looking at her for the first time. Or perhaps it would be better to say he was *seeing* her for the first time!

176

CHAPTER SIXTEEN

The chatter about the incident only lasted a few days but Adam had to admit to himself he was rather glad when it ceased, for he was constantly teased about it. Marie had driven off the next morning, according to the hotel receptionist, in a 'flaming temper', so Adam had her off his back! But instead of it being a relief, in a way it was a nuisance for now Charon had replaced Marie. Adam found himself frequently thinking about her, touched because she had so quickly leapt to his defence, recognising in her action her youth and immaturity, yet feeling he should do something in return to help her.

After all, she had admitted to him her terrible problem, had discussed it with him, and how had he helped her? Simply told her to let time take over, that everything would be all right 'one day'. Talk about passing the buck, Adam told himself impatiently. It was a wonder Charon had any faith in him at all. Somehow or other, he must find a way to help her be able to accept her mother and her mother's action in 'giving her babies away', as Charon still saw it.

But then Nature stepped in and all thoughts left Adam's mind but the urgent necessity of coping with the two minor but frightening epidemics that cropped up, filling the hospital, demanding every moment of the several doctors' time, causing old Dr. Bray to fret and fume because he was tied to his bed, so as to speak, when he should have been out helping.

Amoebic dysentry was the first trouble, then the threat that typhoid was around. Everyone seemed to have the symptoms to be expected and Adam's chances of sleep grew more and more slender, as he drove from house to house, and back to the hospital.

Vaguely he knew that Robin and Mrs. Mortlake had returned to Durban, that Charon was staying on, that Keith was much better, that fortunately the weather was good, no excessive rain and slippery skid-hazardous roads. But most of his time, he was too busy coping with his work to have time to worry about Charon and her inability to accept what her mother had been forced to do.

He was startled one day as the things began to come back to normal and his surgery was no longer crammed with waiting patients, to find Eleanor Lillington walk into his office.

Adam jumped up from this seat. 'You should have 'phoned,' he said. 'It's Keith . . . ?'

She smiled without it reaching her eyes and sat down.

'No, Adam, it's me.'

'You?' He was startled. Eleanor had always seemed so self-possessed, so much in control of herself and her life, that to see her eyes fill up with tears was disconcerting. 'Tell me . . .' he said gently, swinging his chair round, straddling it, and looking at her.

Eleanor dabbed at her eyes, swallowed nervously before speaking. 'I wondered if you could let me have some tranquilisers, Adam. I . . . I'm reaching the end of my tether. I've never felt like this before . . . No, that's not quite true . . .' she went on, her face thoughtful. 'I did feel like this when Tim . . . when Tim was sick and the twins were babies. I keep waiting for something to explode. I don't know what. I'm so tense. My hands shake at times . . .' She looked at him appealingly: 'They've never done that before. I keep crying . . . I . . . I think I hide it successfully for I don't want to upset her . . .'

'Charon?'

Eleanor nodded. 'It's not her fault, it's all mine but . . .'

'I think she's finding it as hard as you . . .'

Adam got up and went to the window, allowing himself a moment's breathing space as he watched the walking patients strolling over the lawn and arguing with the African women selling oranges and fruit.

'Perhaps it would be better if she went away,' Adam said quietly, turning to watch the effect of his words.

Eleanor jumped up. 'Oh, no, then she'd never come back . . .'

It was not quite the reaction he'd expected.

'You want her to understand why you did it?'

He frowned. 'Look, Eleanor, I think the whole situation has been blown up out of all proportions. Lots of mothers, especially young ones, have their children adopted, not because they don't love them but because they *do*. Because they feel they can't give their children as good a chance in life as adoptive parents who have been longing for the privilege of having a child of their own for years. You did nothing wrong. There's absolutely no reason for you to feel guilt. You were advised by people older than yourself—you felt you had no alternative.'

Eleanor had sat down, was resting her chin on her hand, her eyes half-shut. 'I had no alternative,' she said dully. 'Charon would have been . . .' She paused and he saw the tip of her tongue run over her lips. 'Would have died.'

'After all,' Adam went on, vaguely aware that somewhere in what she had said lay a clue, yet unable to pursue it at that moment. 'Your husband was very sick, wasn't he.'

Eleanor buried her face in her hands. 'Very sick, indeed.'

'What sort of man was he?' Adam went on, going to the window again to look out. 'You must have loved him very much to fight your parents and his and elope . . .'

Eleanor lowered her hands. 'I sometimes wonder if I would have married him if they

180

hadn't all been against him. You see, Adam, everyone was against him. Right from the time he was born. His mother died and his father never forgave him for it. Oh, he never said so, of course, but Tim knew. His sister was the same. She was much older than Tim, about seventeen years older, and she had to leave school and stay home and run the house and hated him for it. She always said that was why she'd never married, because of Tim. He was so unhappy and so . . . so unsure of himself . . .' Eleanor's eyes were half-closed as she thought back.

'I was a rebel, you see, Adam, a sort of female Robin Hood.' She laughed unhappily. 'I saw myself saving Tim, building up his morale, reform . . .' She stopped abruptly. 'He was lonely and unhappy, Adam, and I felt I was his only hope. I was young and strong and full of self-confidence. What I didn't realise was that a leopard can't change his spots.'

Adam sat down, glancing surreptitiously at his watch. There were probably patients waiting to be seen, and he was due back at the hospital in half an hour. If only he had more time . . .

'It must have been very difficult when you became pregnant. Rather a shock to you both, Eleanor.'

'Oh, it was, I thought Tim had gone out of his mind . . .' It was her turn to jump up, to walk to the window, talking over her shoulder.

'Some men are born to be parents, others want their wives to themselves. Tim was one of those. He was furious about it, blamed me for it, of course. He said that a baby could destroy our marriage and he'd have no reason left for living. I knew he was thinking that his father had blamed him for killing his mother . . . that perhaps the baby would kill me and . . . and he'd have no one.'

She turned round. 'I didn't want the baby either for it made everything so complicated. You see, I'd had to get a job to keep us and . . .' She sighed. 'It wasn't an easy time.'

'But when the twins were born . . . ?'

Eleanor sat down and smiled at him. 'I adored them. Of course you're used to the miracle of motherhood, Adam, but it was absolutely wonderful.'

'I know. I've seen many a mother who was determined to get rid of her child as soon as possible, suddenly change her mind when the baby's put in her arms.'

'You can't help it. It's knowing they're a part of you, that for nine months they've been utterly dependent on you, that they still need you . . .'

'But of course, the father doesn't feel this,' Adam said drily. 'Your motherhood protective instinct is there and has nothing to do with your own feelings. Just as a hen automatically protects her chicks, or a lioness her cubs, so does a mother automatically love her baby.

182

But to a man, it is quite different. He'll love that child as it grows older and knows him but here at the beginning, I don't think a man has any natural reaction, except perhaps to feel that he now has to share his wife with this whimpering creature and that life will always be different now.'

Eleanor smiled. 'Well put, Adam. I guess that's how poor Tim felt. Girlie, as we called her, was always crying and it was a nuisance for Tim couldn't sleep or study but . . . it wasn't *her* fault . . . and then . . .'

Her face clouded over and her mouth became a thin hard line, as if biting back words that mustn't be said. Adam waited and finally Eleanor unzipped her mouth and said:

'Then Tim was sick and . . . and I knew we could no longer keep the babies.' She sounded unutterably tired. 'It wasn't an easy decision to make, Adam. It hurt me far more than mere words can tell but I had to do it. What upsets me now is that Charon can't keep from believing that I rejected her. And Robin, of course. I can't bear that. Somehow Charon must be made to understand that it broke my heart to part with her, that I loved her then just as I do now . . . just as it's breaking my heart now . . .' Eleanor swallowed nervously. 'If only I knew what to do, Adam . . .'

He scribbled on his prescription pad. Tore off the small sheet and gave it to her. 'Take these, Eleanor, and . . . and I'll have a talk with

Charon. I know she wants to feel like that . . . I mean, to understand your action, just as badly. She's very fond of you, Eleanor, very very fond . . .'

Eleanor's face brightened. 'You think she is?'

'I know she is, she told me so. She's also terrifically sorry for you and very angry with herself but it's something . . .'

'I know. I think I'd feel the same if I suddenly learned that I'd been adopted.'

She stood up and Adam walked with her to the door.

'You know I think the real tragedy is the fact that the Webbs didn't tell her,' Adam said.

Eleanor looked at him. 'You think that would have helped?'

Adam nodded. 'She'd have grown up with the knowledge. This sudden knowledge was a brutal shock. If things don't improve, Eleanor, I think I'll persuade Charon to have psychiatric treatment. I'm not qualified for it but . . .'

'I think you could help Charon more than any psychiatrist,' Eleanor told him as she opened the door. 'You see, she has faith in you, she listens to what you say . . .'

Adam had no chance to think about the conversation until that evening. He sat on the stoep, cradling a glass of Scotch in his hands, frowning down into it.

There must be a clue somewhere. If Charon

184

could only be made to see that Eleanor had had the babies adopted *against* her wish, because she had no other choice. Adam was sure that Tim was the clue . . . Now he remembered the clue he'd been too busy to follow at the time. What was it Eleanor had said?

He frowned, racking his brain and then got it.

'Tim . . .' No, that wasn't it . . . 'Charon would have been . . .' Eleanor had begun and then had stopped and had altered her words to ' . . . Would have died.'

'Had Tim been . . .?' Adam's mind boggled at the thought. But if so, that would explain Eleanor's refusal to talk about Tim's 'Illness', because she would have hated to have to admit to the twins that there might be insanity . . .

Adam drained his glass, refilled it and went to sit down by his father. These evening talks were usually something of an ordeal as the old man was in a temper and still furious with himself for being ill.

But tonight Adam had questions to ask and some of the old Doctor's bad temper vanished as his interest was caught.

'Tim . . .? Let's see, his name was Tim Drake. The Drakes lived here, I remember meeting them once. Let's see . . .' Henry Bray thought carefully. 'We were living at Heidelburg at the time, Adam, and I heard about an opening up here. That was about

185

twenty years ago . . . I remember coming up and being rather shocked by the gossip people seemed to enjoy . . .'

'What were Tim's people like?' Adam asked.

'Well, let me see. There was a spinster sister who had an acid tongue and was disliked by everyone. I say spinster for though she was only in her early thirties, she acted and dressed like a woman of fifty. Always moaning, complaining about things and getting folks into trouble. Not a nice piece of work at all.'

'And the father?'

'A hypocritical swine. A tall gaunt man who believed in hell fire and brimstone, whatever that may mean. A man who saw black as black and white as white, and no greys. There was talk that he whipped his son every Sunday, believing it to be good for him, like giving the boy a . . .'

'Look, Dad, you met Drake?'

'Oh, yes, he was on the hospital board and I gather, voted against me.'

'Would you say . . . was he . . .' Adam paused, seeking the right word.

His father frowned. 'No, he wasn't. Just a . . . a swine. A sadist, perhaps, for he gave his daughter a rotten life, too. Very demanding, arrogant. I don't doubt his constant cruelty was the reason for Tim's drinking . . .'

'Tim drank?' Adam was conscious of a wave of relief that suddenly flooded him.

The older doctor laughed. 'Drink? And how! The only way he found life bearable, I gather.'

'Did they talk about Eleanor?'

'Of course. But Eleanor and her parents came from Quibqo, about forty miles away. Down south. She'd known Tim before but they got really pally while at the same university and fell in love. Everyone was shocked. I reckon that was why she married him.'

'Mind?' Adam asked as he pulled out his cigarette case. 'Like one?'

His father nodded. They sat back for a moment, both smoking contentedly. 'Eleanor came to see me. She's having a bad time. They're both trying so hard and failing.'

The old doctor looked thoughtful. 'I reckon it was because of Tim she had those kids adopted. I had heard he often got violent . . .'

'That's it . . .' Adam smote his thigh. 'That's it, Dad. Eleanor covers for Tim the whole time. She's a loyal soul. She began to say "Charon would have been . . ." and then changed it. I bet you that was what it was. She was afraid Tim would kill the children . . . or perhaps, the child that kept crying. Now if Charon knew that . . .'

'Eleanor would never tell her. That I'm sure. She always was a loyal girl. I remember at the time the people saying how mean they thought her parents were and how Eleanor always stood up for them and said it was her choice to marry Tim and her fault, not theirs.'

'But if Charon was told . . .'

'She'd never believe it. She'd need proof.'

Adam sighed. 'And how can I produce that?'

The old doctor scratched his bald head, patting the few wisps he hated and which his wife refused to cut off.

'Just a moment, son . . .'

Adam waited patiently. He was conscious of a warm glow of happiness for one bogey had been slain. It wouldn't be so bad to know your father drank heavily, especially when you knew that it was because of his unhappy home background and his sense of loneliness.

Dr. Bray looked up. 'I think I've got it, Adam. Old Drake died a few years back but Tim's sister is still alive. She has an arts and crafts shop in Joko, that's about twenty miles away, towards the northern border.'

Adam leant forward. 'But she'd never talk . . .'

'Wouldn't she?' the old man chuckled. 'I bet she would. Just ask about brother Tim and you'll get a gush of vitriolic hatred of Tim that would shock Charon but also give her some idea of what her mother had to put up with . . .'

'You mean? That Charon should meet Tim's sister?'

'Exactly. Her aunt!'

'You don't think it would be too great a shock . . . I mean to hear your father spoken of . . .'

'Charon will move in to protect him, to find a reason for his drunkenness, this will help her forgive him for behaving as he did, help her rationalize it so that she sees that he didn't hate her . . . as a person, but as part of his unhappy make-up.'

Adam stared at the old man. 'You know, I think you've got something there, Dad.'

The old man beamed. 'At least one member of our family has some brains . . .'

Adam grinned. 'You're so right.'

Then the older man's face grew grave. 'You're getting pretty involved, aren't you, Adam? You haven't fallen in love with Eleanor, by any chance?'

Adam showed his surprise. 'Eleanor? Good grief, no, why I like her but . . .'

'Then is it Charon?'

'Charon—She's just a kid. You haven't met her, have you, Dad?'

'No, I haven't, son. I'd like to. I'll get your mother to ask her up for tea. A fresh face is always a delight. What's she like?'

'Who? Charon? Oh, well . . .' Adam considered the question for a moment. 'She's not pretty nor is she beautiful but . . . well, it's a rather fascinating face. Her hair is dark, like Eleanor's, and cut short. When I first saw her it was long and braided round her head. Made her look ten years or more older. She's tall, very tall for a girl and like her mother, has very

189

dark eyes but . . . well, she lacks Eleanor's go-aheadness, her suppressed energy. Robin, the other twin, is much more like Eleanor, physically and mentally than Charon.'

'That could be environment.'

'I agree. She's very loyal but rather . . . well, how shall I put it? Disciplined. She's ashamed of herself if she does anything that doesn't conform to her upbringing and gets very upset if she thinks she's hurt anyone. That's the tragedy of it all. Eleanor hurts Charon by showing how upset she is—and Charon hurts Eleanor by showing how upset *she* is. It's a sort of vicious circle . . .'

The door opened and Mrs. Bray stood there, pulling off her gloves, pretending to frown.

'Now see what happens when I'm out,' she scolded. 'Both of you should be asleep by now . . .'

Adam stood up. 'I could do with some right now. Thanks, Dad, you've helped a lot . . .'

'I certainly hope so, son,' the older man said, watching him go, turning to his wife with a smile. 'Have a good meeting . . . ?'

'Absolutely fine. Everyone lost their temper and some truths were heard, at last. Like a cup of coffee . . . ?'

He smiled. 'I'd like a Scotch if you could bring yourself not to notice it.'

She bent and kissed him. 'I guess you deserve it. Adam been weeping on your

190

shoulder?'

'No, just asking questions about Eleanor and her husband . . .'

He saw his wife's eyes brighten with interest. 'But why? And what about?'

'Oh, just questions. I'm longing for that drink.'

'I'm on my way,' she promised and left the room.

Adam came back to stand in the doorway.

'Dad, one thing worries me.'

His father yawned. 'Lot's of things worry me, son, but they all get sorted out. Look out, your Mum's nose is quivering. We don't want it all over town that you're asking questions about Eleanor's first husband, do we?'

Adam grinned back. 'Too right, we don't, Dad. 'Night.'

' 'Night,' the old doctor said and closed his eyes. Adam would find a way. There always was a way if you *sought* hard enough.

CHAPTER SEVENTEEN

The days were dragging for Charon. She missed Robin's gay company and Aunt Irene's understanding more than she had expected. The children were back at school, the weather perfect, and there was nothing to do.

Except keep out of 'Ma's' way as much as

possible, Charon thought miserably. They got on perfectly on the surface but it was an unnatural sort of friendliness, a tense situation as if both were waiting for something to happen, something that they both hoped would never happen.

Her first surprise came when Adam's mother asked Eleanor and Charon up to tea. Of course Mrs. Bray and 'Ma' were old friends, both sitting on the same committees, both sharing the same interests. Charon was rather startled when Adam's mother, who seemed very nice and friendly, asked her if she would mind going to meet Adam's father.

'He's finding it a bind to be tied to his bed,' Mrs. Bray said with a smile. 'And he says he gets tired of familiar faces. Maybe you could chat to him for a while, Charon? It would be a favour.'

'Of course,' Charon said but she went to the old doctor's bedroom rather nervously. What would they talk about, she wondered.

She need not have worried for the old doctor did most of the talking. Propped up in bed by innumerable cushions, he looked pale and sometimes tired but his eyes were full of interest and he laughed a lot. He asked lots of questions, too, and Charon found herself relaxing more and more as they talked. He was interested in her life at the Convent Orphanage and asked if she knew of any of the children who had left and got married.

'I'm thinking of writing a book,' he told her. 'About orphaned children, or children from broken homes in orphanages, and how they react to marriage. Are they afraid to marry? Afraid of getting hurt as their parents must have been hurt . . .'

He asked questions about the Webbs and it was quite nostalgic she found to remember those wonderfully happy days.

He talked of Robin, said he wished he'd met him. 'But doubtless he'll be coming up in the holidays.'

'I'm not sure,' Charon told him and then found herself telling him all about Robin's love for Tess. 'I just can't understand how you can fall in love with a person in . . . well, in a day or so.'

'Oh, you can,' the old doctor said gravely. 'I did—with my wife. But every person loves differently. Now some would take a long time, would need to know the person well. What's young Robin doing about it? I mean if they're both students.'

'I know, that's the trouble. Robin feels that students shouldn't marry for it isn't fair on their children.'

'That's not such a problem today,' the old doctor said. 'You can postpone parenthood . . .'

'There can still be accidents,' Charon said. 'At the hostel we often had unmarried mothers there and lots said how shocked they were, as

193

they were sure they were "all right".'

'That's true,' Dr. Bray sighed. 'So Robin's giving up his girl friend?'

'Oh no, they decided to get unofficially engaged and go back to their universities and then meet next hols and see how they felt.'

'And how d'you think they will feel?'

Charon laughed. 'I'm wondering. I had a letter the other day from Robin and he says that Tess is very bossy and he's not sure he likes it . . . It seems she writes him long letters and is furious if he doesn't write equally long ones back.'

Dr. Bray chuckled. 'Well, well, well. The problem, Charon, is that a man and woman each see marriage differently. And parenthood,' he went on, carefully keeping his voice casual. 'Very few fathers experience the same love for their children while they are babies as the mother does. The baby is infinitely more important and more precious to the mother than to the father. He feels, well, how shall I put it? Rather outside, shall we say? Jealous, perhaps. Resentful.'

Charon looked puzzled. 'You mean a man doesn't love his baby?'

'No, perhaps that's too strong. Shall we say that the baby is an impersonal thing to a man, not a part of him as the baby is to her mother. That's why fathers, particularly young ones who resent this intrusion into their lives, sometimes seem to hate their babies. They don't really hate them, they just have to get adjusted, and really, deep down inside them, there is love waiting for that child, when that child is old enough to receive it.'

'I don't understand.'

Dr. Bray gave a little laugh. 'It's not easy to explain. What I'm trying to say is, that a child shouldn't be hurt if he finds his father didn't love him when he was a baby.'

Charon moved uneasily. This was rather beyond her, she thought. What was Dr. Bray trying to say? Was he perhaps feeling guilty about Adam? Had he been horrid to Adam when Adam was a baby and was this worrying him, now? But why tell her, Charon wondered and was grateful when the door opened suddenly and Mrs. Bray stood there smiling.

'I'm afraid visiting time is over . . .'

'This is absurd. I am not an ill man . . .' Dr. Bray began angrily but his wife, smiling at Charon, deftly led her out of the room, closing the door behind her.

'He mustn't get tired, you see, Charon, but he isn't easy to handle.'

'Is Adam like this when he's ill?' Charon asked as they went back to the stoep where they'd had tea.

Mrs. Bray chuckled. 'Surprisingly enough, he is. One has to almost use handcuffs to the bed rails to keep Adam in bed. Men!' she said, as if the word explained everything.

It was much later, sitting in an awkward

silence by her mother's side, that Charon remembered the rather extraordinary words Mrs. Bray had used. 'Surprisingly enough'.

About a week later, Charon had another surprise. Adam 'phoned her. She was quite startled when the housegirl came running out to the pool to say there was a 'phone call for the Young Missis and that it was the Doctor.

'Charon here . . .' she said into the mouthpiece and Adam's voice came clear and sure in her ear.

'Charon, I need your help. Could you be ready in fifteen minutes if I pick you up?'

She thought fast. 'Ma' was out but she could leave her a note for there wasn't time to go and look for Sam who was somewhere in the orchards.

'Of course,' she said.

Adam seemed to hesitate. 'Charon, I wonder if you'd mind wearing a . . . a nurse's uniform? I'll bring it round and . . .'

She was certain now that he needed her help with some 'difficult' child; probably the uniform was to create extra respect.

'Of course I don't mind. But Adam, remember I'm very tall . . .' she added.

He laughed. 'You don't feel a mini-mini-skirt would be appropriate.'

'Hardly.'

'Oh, and not much make-up, Charon, just as if you'd come off the wards. In the Convent,' he added and she could imagine him smiling.

She wrote the note and stood it against the telephone, hurried to her room and washed her face first, carefully removing all make-up, brushing her hair so that it looked softer, and wondering what she'd look like in nurse's uniform.

Adam arrived and sat outside, impatiently waiting while she changed. She didn't look too bad, she thought, as she stared in the mirror. The uniform, especially the cap, made her look quite different.

Adam nodded in approval when she joined him. 'Where are we going,' she asked.

'A place called Joko.' He drove down the road that led to the main one. 'You made a big impression on Dad.'

'I liked him but oh, how he does talk,' Charon said with a laugh.

'He's glad of the chance to get a listener. These days, his life is pretty bleak. What did you talk about . . .?' He swung the wheel round to get on the main road. He hoped he wouldn't get lost. He'd certainly studied the map and the signposts would show the way. The trouble was, he felt nervous. He wasn't at all sure if this was the right way to handle it. It could be a pretty bad shock for Charon.

'Talked about everything,' she told Adam. 'Marriage, Robin, oh, and parenthood. Adam, he seems to have rather a thing about something. He kept saying that a baby doesn't mean as much to the father as to the mother.

Yet, he said, that later on, the father can love the child as it grows up just as much as the mother can. It didn't make sense.'

The road wound up the mountainside, they had to go down into the next valley and then follow the river, Adam reminded himself. There were tall gum trees either side of the road, and the usual huge rocks which looked as if they'd been tossed about by some giant impatient hand.

'I think it does, Charon. You see, the baby belongs much more to the mother at the beginning. He's so dependant on her. He's not at all dependant on father and I think that riles some men. Also they can be jealous, can feel the child has stolen the wife . . .'

'It sounds crazy to me. After all, the child is his and surely he should feel love as well as a sense of responsibility . . .'

'What you should do and what you do do are two very different things, Charon,' Adam said, relaxing slightly as he drove up the winding road. 'Take me, for instance. I'm adopted, you know.'

'You're not?' Charon cried in amazement. She tucked her long legs under her and turned on the seat to look at him. 'Everyone suddenly seems to be adopted. Robin and me. Sam. Only he wasn't actually adopted, his father's best friend looked after him which I think was pretty super of him. And now you!'

Adam smiled. 'You'd probably be amazed

how many people *are* adopted. You see, one doesn't go round wearing a label or shouting: Watch out, I'm adopted. If you're properly adopted, you're bursting with pride because you were "chosen".'

'That's what Robin said. Now I know why your mother . . . I mean, Mrs. Bray . . .'

'No, Charon, she's my mother all right. Even if we're not related by blood. She's the only mother I've had and she's been wonderful in every way. What did she say?'

'Oh, she was saying how difficult it was to keep . . . to keep your father in bed and I asked if you were just as difficult and she said: "Surprisingly enough he is,". I wondered at the time what she meant but now I understand.'

The road had passed over the top of the mountain and now they were driving through miles and miles of pines in the enormous man-made forest. Adam could vaguely smell the pines.

'Well, I was adopted for a strange reason,' Adam went on. 'You see, I was about a month old when my mother died, my father had died a month before in a train smash. I imagine my mother's shock caused the premature birth and her death. Anyhow, one day as I lay, a small baby of three months, quite happy, apparently a couple came to see me. Their name was Crabbe.'

'Crabbe?' Charon asked.

Adam lifted her hand. 'Let me go on. Well,

199

finally the Crabbes took me home. You know there is quite a long probation period. A month after they got me, Frederick Crabbe walked out on his wife.'

'Walked out?'

'Yes. Apparently their marriage had been rather chaotic for years. He was always away from home for months on end and she was lonely. She wanted a child but the doctors had said he couldn't have one. Not unnaturally this infuriated him for most men, foolishly or not, consider it a terrible humiliating thing to be sterile. Personally I think they make too much of it. It's nothing to be ashamed of. Anyhow, Frederick suggested they adopted a child and rather reluctantly, his wife agreed. She was a lonely unhappy woman and she knew that when he was away for months on end, it had nothing to do with his work. Anyhow, as I said, he walked out and she was left with me. She had, by then, apparently, taken rather a fancy to me . . .' Adam smiled at Charon, 'And couldn't bear the thought of consigning me back to the austere cleanliness of the Home. So she moved away and got a job, putting me in a baby's clinic. She had a battle about money and the adoption authorities traced her down and threatened to take the boy—that was me—back. Then the old man walked in. Only he wasn't old, then. He was a young doctor who'd just been given a wonderful opportunity to go to South America on a medical research survey. This was something he fought to get and now he'd got it only he met up with Mum. When I say "met up", it doesn't make sense.

'They'd known one another for years, off and on, more often off than on, if you get me, for though both came from the same small town, their lives had separated. Apparently Dad had always carried the torch for Mum but she had married the other man. Now Dad found she was free, for the divorce had gone through and he asked her to marry him, but that he would be away for six or seven months. It was then that the adoption people put down a stern foot and said it was out of the question. If he married my mother and would be resident in the country, then they could adopt me. If he was going to be away for long periods, then the child must go back to the Home. So Dad gave up the research chance and settled down to being a G.P.'

'That was wonderful of him,' Charon said quietly.

Adam glanced at her. 'It certainly was. He never told me but Mum did. I've never forgotten it.'

'No wonder you're a dutiful son . . .'

He turned, his face angry. 'But I'm not. I mean, I didn't decide to settle up here because of Dad. I swear I didn't, Charon. Don't give me virtues I don't possess. I decided to settle here because I like the life, because I'm happy here, because . . .'

'You won't have Marie chasing *you*.' Charon finished for him.

He laughed. 'Oh, I think she got the message this time. By the way, have I ever thanked you for standing up for me? If not, then thanks, Charon.'

'I didn't stand up for *you*,' she told him quickly. 'I stood up for the truth. She was telling lies and I knew it could harm you.'

'I see . . .' He tried not to smile. 'What you mean is that there wasn't anything personal about it? It wasn't because it was me . . .? That's right.'

'Yes, that's right . . .' Charon sounded puzzled. 'You make it so involved.'

'No, I don't. You'd stand up for anyone, even if you hated them, if you believed they were being treated unfairly. Is that right?'

She frowned. 'Yes, I . . . well, I suppose it is. I just don't like lies or people being hurt.'

She wondered why Adam looked so pleased. He began to whistle and the car slowed down as they drove between the neat rows of small houses of the African township. Small piccanins were racing round in the dust, a few African women in voluminous Mother-Hubbard frocks were hoeing the dry ground and then they reached the small town. It was barely fifty yards of street with a store, a post office, a garage, a hotel and a weird-looking shop. Hanging over the door, was a rocking chair. Printed in big letters that needed repainting, they read

ESTHER DRAKE. ANTIQUES.

Adam parked the car, and opened the door for Charon.

'We've got to go into that shop, Charon. This has to be handled with diplomacy. I want you to go inside behind me and then turn and look at some of the things for sale. Try not to look at the woman behind the counter. Just keep quiet while I talk.'

'Is she difficult?' she asked wondering why he looked so tense.

'I gather she is very difficult,' he said grimly. 'Just say nothing but listen to what she says and promise me one thing, Charon . . .' He looked at her gravely. 'And I mean this. Promise me you won't speak. No matter what I say or what she says, promise you won't interrupt or say a thing. When I've finished, I'll turn round to you and then you can say anything you like. Is that a promise? It may not be easy.'

'Yes, I promise,' she said. 'But I don't understand.'

'You will,' he told her, holding her arm firmly but letting it go as he went to open the door of the shop. It was dark and fusty-smelling inside, filled with furniture and china and weird-looking ornaments on the shelves.

As she had promised, Charon let him go ahead and as soon as she was in the shop, she

203

turned and concentrated her interest on a beautifully-carved small desk. What was it all about, she wondered. Had this woman some sick children and had she refused to call a doctor? What was *her* part, Charon wondered. Whatever it was, she was prepared to help Adam. She was only grateful he'd asked for her help. Her days were so empty that it was wonderful to be 'wanted', even if only for an hour.

Then she got the shock of a lifetime as she heard Adam say:

'Miss Drake? I wonder if you could tell me where your brother, Tim is? I've not been around but I understand—he married Eleanor some twenty years ago . . .'

'Tim . . .?' A cold voice echoed. 'Is it my brother, Tim, you're asking after? And what would you want with him? You're a friend of his, you say? I doubt if he had a friend in the whole world. He was the scum of the earth and so was she . . .'

Charon closed her eyes tightly. For a moment, she felt suffocated. This must be her aunt. Her father's sister. But what a terrible woman she sounded. Why, she thought miserably, why have you done this to me, Adam?

CHAPTER EIGHTEEN

Adam stood very still, fighting the desire to close his ears as Esther Drake talked. Now he knew what his father had meant when he called her tongue 'vitriolic'! How the hatred, built up over the years, and the embittered resentment was spilling out, her gaunt face red, eyes flashing, long fingers clenched into fists as she talked as if she wished to use them.

'It was all that woman's fault . . .' Esther Drake went on, her voice rasping like a saw. 'He should never have married her. It was all her fault. She made him. There's no doubt about that! He hadn't the guts to defy Dad on his own. No, she made him all right, and they just students. What sort of marriage could that be, I ask you. Doomed before it began. And then she has to go and have twins. I ask you! And Tim a student, working like a slave in the holidays to earn money, studying every night and kept awake by those wailing kids. Though I blame him for being foolish enough to do what Eleanor wanted, yet I felt sorry for him for what he had to suffer. How can you study when a kid squalls all the time. It nearly drove him mad and I'm not surprised. If there's one thing I can't abide, it's a baby screaming . . .'

Esther Drake paused for breath and Adam had to fight another desire, this time to turn and hold Charon tightly in his arms, to comfort her, to reassure her that all people were not like her aunt, to apologise and try to explain Esther Drake's viciousness was due to embitterment, but he knew he must not move. Now Esther had started her diatribe, she must finish it. Poor Charon had to hear it all—it was the only way to cure her feeling of having been rejected by her mother, the only way to make her understand that Eleanor had no choice.

'What sort of man was Tim?' Adam prompted quietly. 'I know so little about him.'

Esther, a tall gaunt woman in old-fashioned clothes, stared at him. 'You didn't lose much. He never was much good, in my opinion. He killed my mother. I was seventeen when he was born and Mum was old. Too old to have a child. She died when Tim was born and I had to leave school and run the house. How I hated him for it. It ruined my life all right, you could almost say he killed me for I had no chance to get married or do anything I wanted to. He killed Dad, too, having that dreadful motor-bike crash and being so drunk. The papers were full of it. We nearly died of shame, Tim being one of the family. He had no friends. None at all. At school he wasn't much good . . .'

'But he managed to get to the university?'

'Oh yes, he could study when he wanted anything bad enough.'

'I rather gathered he'd known Eleanor for

some time before they got married.'

'Oh yes, he knew her all right. She was the only girl who'd ever go out with him. He even brought her home. We didn't like her much. Too bossy and sure of herself, always laughing and talking a lot. Everyone was against the marriage so then they go and elope. Of course, Dad could have stopped it and so could her parents for they were under-age, but we knew if we did that, they'd only elope again and so it would go on.'

'How long were they married,' he asked casually, 'before the twins were born?'

'How long? I don't know. I didn't live with them. About a year or eighteen months, I'd say. Of course, having twins was really the end. Poor Tim couldn't take any more. There was he, working hard in the holidays to earn money and in the term studying hard and those kids squalling all the time.'

'I understood Eleanor also worked,' Adam said quietly.

'Oh, yes, she had to. They had to live, hadn't they? She sent the kids every day to a clinic or something, I think, I really don't know. One, the girl, I believe, never stopped crying. I don't wonder Tim nearly went round the bend. Then Eleanor went all hysterical one night and screamed and the police came round and what a scandal there was until it was ironed out. It was all a misunderstanding, you see. Tim couldn't sleep and the baby kept screaming and so he covered up the child's face with a pillow, just to make the noise less loud and Eleanor, waking up, saw him and thought he was smothering the child and so she screamed. Typical of her, jumping to conclusions and acting impulsively. Anyhow maybe it was a good thing for the doctors made them have the kids adopted. They should have done it at once, as soon as the kids were born, I always said.'

Adam managed to keep his voice steady. 'Of course he was only trying to sleep.'

'Of course. He wouldn't have killed the child. He hadn't the guts to kill a fly, even. No, he just naturally wanted to sleep and the kid wouldn't let him, so . . .'

'I gathered the baby was delicate and always ill . . .'

'Yes, a proper little nuisance.'

'You didn't live with them. Did you visit them a lot?'

'Me? Visit them? Of course not. After the twins went, Eleanor was sick and in hospital. Nerves they said, just wanting to be made a fuss of, I said. Her parents were dead and she only had Tim, so although he came and stayed with us while she was in hospital, as soon as she was out, she came and got him. He told us about the twins and how they cried and they only had two rooms and the place was full of flapping wet nappies and baby clothes. Nearly drove him mad, poor lad.'

'As I remember it,' Adam said drily, 'Tim drank rather a lot.'

'Drink? I'll say he did! That's what upset my father so when he died. We were really ashamed. Not one of us drank! We've always been teetotal.'

'I wonder why he drank . . .' Adam said slowly. He wanted to look over his shoulder and see how poor Charon was taking it but decided not to.

'Who can say?' Esther Drake asked, shrugging her thin bony shoulders. 'He said once it was because he was lonely. Who wasn't? The dear Lord knows I was lonely enough but I didn't take to the bottle. Just weak, that's what he was, a weakling,' she said scornfully. 'But it was all her fault, mind, if it hadn't been for her, he'd have been alive today.'

'But he drank before he was married, didn't he?'

'Oh sure, but she was always on at him to stop drinking and that never works. Now does it? Tell a man not to drink and he'll go and get drunk just to show you how unimportant you are. I gathered at the inquest—there was all that publicity, you know, really shameful—that they'd had a row and some of the witnesses said Tim had knocked Eleanor down but that I don't believe. Anyway, he was drunk and drove straight into a tree. I guess he felt he couldn't take any more of a bossy wife . . .'

Adam felt the moment had come to leave. 'Thank you very much, Miss Drake. I'm most grateful to you . . .'

She stared at him, her thick dark brows lifted, her gaunt checks flushed. 'You don't want to buy anything? Wasting all my time, talking like that, and you . . .'

Before Adam could answer, he felt a movement by his side. Charon was there, her face white, her hands shaking as she laid two dollars on the counter.

'Thank you,' she said quietly. 'You've been a great help . . .'

Esther Drake stared at her, the blood leaving her cheeks for the moment, her eyes huge and then her fury exploded.

'Why, you're the dead spitting image of Eleanor . . .'

'Yes, she's my mother,' Charon said quietly. 'And you are my aunt.'

'Get out of here . . . if you think you're getting any money from me, you're mistaken. Dad left it all to me . . . there's none for you . . .' Esther Drake was almost screaming, flailing her arms about.

Charon turned away and looked at Adam. 'Could we go home, now?' she said quietly and led the way out of the shop.

She sat silently by his side as he drove her home. As he drove up outside the farmhouse, she glanced at him.

'Please don't come in, if you don't mind,

Adam. I want to be alone with Mother.'

He nodded. 'I'm sorry, Charon. Most terribly sorry but . . .'

She smiled, a wry unhappy smile. 'Don't be sorry, Adam. I'm grateful. It was the only way.'

He hesitated. She looked so forlorn, poor child.

'Don't blame your father too much, Charon. He was a very unhappy young man, with a terrible background.'

'I won't blame him,' she said, her voice tired. 'Now I know why your father went to such trouble to make me understand that men feel differently about their babies than women do.'

'He was unbalanced, neurotic, a drinker. It wasn't all his fault.'

'It certainly wasn't any of it my mother's fault,' Charon said indignantly.

Adam smiled. 'So now we see eye to eye. Charon . . .' he began but she was scrambling out of the car and when she turned to slam the door, he saw that she was very near tears.

'Please don't come in, Adam,' she begged. 'Please . . .'

He watched her run indoors, then reversed his car and drove back to the hospital. He would have a lot to tell the old man that night . . .

But as usual, things didn't work out as he had planned. A bridge under construction had collapsed and about twenty workmen had been admitted to the hospital, half of them seriously ill. There was work to be done and no time to chatter, with little chance of sleep and it was nearly three days before Adam found time to draw a long breath and think of life outside.

He immediately rang Eleanor. 'I just wondered . . .' he began. But she interrupted him.

'I don't know how to thank you, Adam, you and your father. I'd have rung you earlier but I understood everything has been pretty chaotic for you.'

'It certainly has. How is she? Charon, I mean. I was a bit worried. It must have been a terrible shock, a ghastly experience to hear that woman talking like that. I was so afraid we might be doing the wrong thing.'

'I don't think you need be afraid of that, Adam,' Eleanor said and her voice sounded strange to Adam, as if she would like to say much more. 'Charon was shocked and rather upset, but it was for me. She felt terrible because she had blamed me for everything and now she knew the truth but I think she also was tremendously relieved to realise how much I had loved her as a baby. It was that thought of being rejected by her mother that hurt her most. Your father, too, very cleverly made her see the man's point of view and this helped her understand poor Tim.'

'You can talk about it?'

Eleanor laughed, a happy sound. 'You

should have heard us. She wanted to know everything and it had to be the truth. When we'd finished, I think she had a much better understanding of poor Tim, and perhaps I had, too. Anyhow, everything's fine, Adam, and many thanks.'

'Is . . . could I speak to Charon a moment?' Adam asked, rather diffidently. 'I'm going to Cheki on Sunday and wondered if she'd like to come for the trip.'

'To Cheki?' Eleanor sounded surprised. 'I'm sure she'd love to only she isn't here.'

'Isn't there?' His surprise and something rather like dismay surely sounded in his voice, he thought.

'No, she's gone down to Durban to stay awhile with Irene. We talked it over. We were both very emotional about it, of course. In fact, I suggested it and she jumped at it. I think since she's been here, she's had quite a few shocks . . .'

Once again, Adam heard a strange tone in Eleanor's voice. It sounded as if she knew something but couldn't mention it. Something important but that had to be handled carefully.

'Will she be gone long?' Adam asked, unaware of how forlorn he sounded.

'I don't know, Adam,' Eleanor told him. 'It depends on so many things. It may be weeks, it could be months.'

'Oh, well, when you write, give her my best wishes and I hope she enjoys herself . . .' Adam said lamely.

He replaced the receiver and stared at it miserably. Somehow it had never entered his head that Charon might go away.

CHAPTER NINETEEN

Durban was hot and uncomfortably humid as Charon wandered down West Street idly, trying to be interested in the shops, and failing miserably. As soon as she was alone, no matter how hard she fought it, her thoughts went back to Adam.

How could she have been so blind all this time, she wondered. Right from the beginning, he had been 'different' but somehow, she had not thought that what she felt for him could be 'love'. She had never been sure what that word meant. It seemed as if everyone had a different definition. She had respected Adam, liked him, known she could turn to him in trouble, always been glad to see him—but it wasn't until that awful journey back from Joko that it had hit her. 'Wham!' as Robin would put it.

Normally her life in Durban with Aunt Irene was good fun, it was only when Charon was alone that this unhappy nagging pain began for it was hopeless. No matter what her real mother said, Charon knew that Adam just didn't know she existed.

Charon didn't want to talk about it and though she was sure her mother had told Aunt Irene all about it, Charon was grateful that it had not been mentioned yet. At the moment, poor Aunt Irene was at the dentists, which was why Charon was alone.

She turned back, walked to the Post Office and down towards the sea, remembering that terrible day when Adam had driven her to meet that awful woman . . .

What a fearful shock it had been to hear those vindictive cruel words. How hard Charon had found it to stand still and let them go on, yet she had promised Adam, and in her heart, even while she cringed at the hatred shown, Charon had known she wanted to hear the whole truth. Esther Drake's vicious words had revealed everything to Charon, and she had been filled with shame at her misjudgement of her mother, and sympathy for her. She had felt unable to speak in the car and Adam had seemed to feel the same. They had sat silently, while her thoughts raced backwards and forwards like a small frightened animal. Then suddenly she had known.

Later she had tried to explain to her mother. But first when Adam stopped the car and made to get out, Charon had known she wanted to be alone with her mother, so she'd asked him not to follow her in, and then had raced to find Eleanor. When she did, Charon had acted without thought, rushing to her, flinging her arms round her and bursting into tears.

'Why didn't you tell me about my father?' Charon had sobbed. 'I'd have understood . . .'

'Everyone was against him. I didn't want you and Robin to think ill of him, too,' her mother had said, finally crying, too, as she listened to Charon's story of what had happened.

'My poor darling, Adam shouldn't have done that to you. He'd no right to interfere and hurt you . . .'

'But he did it to help me, Mum . . .' Charon said. Said the word again, liking the sound of it. 'Mum . . . He knew how confused and unhappy I was. He said he was sorry and then . . .' and she'd begun to cry again. 'I knew . . .'

'You knew what?' her mother'd asked gently.

'I knew I loved him,' Charon had confessed. 'And he doesn't even see me,' she wailed.

It had taken them both a long time to stop crying and talk sensibly, then Charon had been amazed by her mother's compassionate understanding of Esther Drake.

'She always hated me, poor girl. You see I personified everything she wanted to be. Try not to blame her too much. She believes what she said, but only because she wants to.'

Charon and her mother had talked frankly about Eleanor's marriage. 'His father and sister were awful to him, Charon. They blamed

216

him for his mother's death, for everything. They publicly humiliated him. I'm sure now that more than half of my love for him was really pity. I wanted him to be happy as I was and I was young enough to think I could help him. I was too late.'

'D'you think he tried to kill me?' Charon asked.

Her mother shook her head. 'No. He was drunk and half asleep. I honestly think he only tried to muffle the sound.' She smiled wryly at Charon. 'Darling, I must confess it was pretty awful, you know. I tried everything to stop you from crying but I just couldn't. You were such an unhappy little thing. In a way, I could see Tim's point of view but it wasn't your fault or mine then . . . then when I woke up and saw Tim putting the pillow over your face, I panicked and screamed . . .'

'Did he often hit you?' Charon felt she wanted to know everything.

'Sometimes. But he was always awfully upset afterwards so I knew it wasn't the real Tim, the Tim I loved, who did such things. But when it came to the babies, that was different. They were helpless. I'm afraid I broke down when the doctor came, and I told him everything and that was why I was advised to have you adopted. He said Tim would never be able to accept you children, that he needed psychiatric treatment and had refused to have it, that I was too young and that it wasn't fair

217

on you children . . . In the end, I gave way. Later when Tim died, I went to try and get you back, but I was told you'd been adopted. If only they'd told me when the Webbs died . . .'

They had talked for hours for there'd been so much to say and both had found it wonderful that the barrier raised between them had gone.

Then they had talked about Adam. 'How long have you known you loved Adam?' Charon's mother had asked quite calmly as if it was the most natural thing in the world.

'I've always liked him a lot but . . . well, I honestly think it was in the car when he brought me back today. I sat there stunned. The things that dreadful woman said! I'd never heard things like that before and I knew they were all lies. She wasn't even human. She said she hated to hear a baby cry. NOT because it worried her to think the child was ill but because it was a nuisance!

'Then, sitting by Adam's side, I wondered how many men, busy as Adam is, would have bothered to spare the time to help a stranger as he'd helped me. I knew he'd hated it, that was easy to see for he stood so tensely and his voice was stiff. He'd done it for me . . .

'And then . . . and then when he said he was sorry, something seemed to hit me and I knew I loved him. Then I realised that to him, I wasn't a woman or even a girl. I was a child and a stranger he was sorry for. That was all.

And I felt I couldn't bear it.'

Her mother had looked at her oddly. 'I wonder if you're right, Charon darling.'

'He never even looks at me.'

'Oh, he does. I've seen him. I think he likes you quite a lot.'

'Likes me . . .' Charon had said despairingly.

'The life of a doctor's wife isn't an easy one, you know. Long hours alone, always taking second place in his life . . .'

'I could do it,' Charon had been very sure. 'But I haven't got a hope. I'm certain he's a dedicated doctor.'

It had been her mother's idea that Charon came down to Durban to stay with Aunt Irene. 'You'll dread seeing Adam in case he realises you love him,' Eleanor had said sympathetically. 'So a few weeks away might help.'

'Yes, it might,' Charon had agreed and then had looked at her mother. 'You wouldn't mind?'

Eleanor had smiled. A lovely smile that needed no words. 'Not now, darling.'

Eleanor drove Charon to the airport and kissed her.

'Not to worry, Charon. Things work out. Maybe when you're not around, Adam will wake up and realise how much he likes you,' she said cheerfully.

Charon had hugged her mother and given a little laugh. 'It couldn't happen,' she'd said rather wistfully, then seen the disappointment on Eleanor's face and added hastily: 'But miracles do happen, sometimes, don't they? They have—to me.'

The flight had been without incident except that it gave Charon too much time to think about Adam, and to feel more and more certain that Adam would neither know or notice that she was no longer there.

Now Charon could see the Indian Ocean ahead of her, blue and sparkling in the sunshine, so she walked along the Front towards the big block of modern flats where Aunt Irene now lived.

'I decided to sell my house and move to a flat, Charon,' she had said as she drove Charon from the airport. 'Once Robin finishes at Uni. he is bound to fly from the nest, and quite right, too, for I want him to see the world before he settles down.'

It was a beautiful flat, luxuriously furnished, with three bedrooms, a lounge and balcony overlooking the ocean, a dining-room, very modern kitchen and a superb bathroom with walls made of mirrors.

'Rather depressing at my age,' Aunt Irene said drily. 'But as the mirrors were there, I had to accept them.'

Charon had been in Durban for two weeks, now. Two long weeks and no sign that Adam had noticed she was gone, she thought unhappily, as the silent lift whisked her eerily up to the tenth floor. Robin had been to see them the previous weekend and had looked uncomfortable when Charon asked him about Tess.

'It isn't working out, Charon,' he admitted. 'Sometimes I can't even remember what she looked like. She writes so often and bullies me because I don't write back but there just isn't anything to say!'

Charon had been rather shocked. 'But you were so much in love with her.'

He'd shrugged his shoulders. 'That's what I thought but I was wrong. Not to worry, Chary. Tess is no fool so she'll get the message in the end.'

'Aren't you being rather callous? Poor Tess,' Charon had said indignantly.

He looked startled. 'What about poor me? It's part of growing-up, Chary. Waking up and realising it was just infatuation and not love.'

Charon wished she could view it so philosophically and as she walked down the corridor with the polished floor, she wondered if one day she would look back on this period of her life with sympathetic amusement. Could she fall out of love with Adam as fast as Robin had fallen out of love with Tess?

As she opened the front door, she heard Aunt Irene on the phone. '. . . Afraid I don't know when she'll be in. Oh, hold on for just a minute, here she is. Charon . . .' Aunt Irene called. 'You're wanted on the 'phone.'

It was probably the Convent, Charon thought as she hurried to the big sunny lounge. Sister Ann had asked her to go up and see a certain sick child after an operation and said she'd phone when it was the right time.

Perhaps Aunt Irene's excitement should have warned Charon but she was completely taken by surprise when she recognised Adam's voice.

'Charon. How are things?' he asked cheerfully.

For a moment she couldn't speak, then she managed a rather squeaky: 'Fine. Where are you?'

'Here, in Durban,' he told her. 'I had to come down, clearing up a few matters, you know. Are you free tonight? I thought it would be nice if we had dinner together and danced afterwards.'

She caught her breath. Adam—asking her to dine and dance? It couldn't be happening. And then she felt sure she knew why, he was still feeling upset about that awful scene with her aunt and wanted to make amends.

'Well . . .' She hesitated. She wanted to go but yet she didn't want him to take her out just because he was sorry for her. How could she refuse without being rude—and really, she didn't want to refuse! 'I can't dance, Adam. Robin says I'm hopeless.'

'Robin's an idiot at times,' Adam said cheerfully. 'I'll call for you at half-past seven.

Actually I'm no dancer, myself, Charon. Marie always said I was like a lumbering elephant for I was always treading on her toes.'

Charon managed to laugh. 'We both sound hopeless. Well, we've been warned.'

'I'm not worried. Maybe we can teach each other. See you later, Charon,' he rang off before she could say any more.

Slowly Charon replaced the receiver. She turned and saw Aunt Irene standing there, her face excited.

'Adam . . . ?'

Charon laughed. 'You spoke to him so you know very well it was Adam.' Suddenly she felt gay and light-hearted. 'He's asked me out to dinner and to dance . . .'

Aunt Irene clapped her hands. 'How marvellous, darling. So your mother was right . . .' Her hand flew to her mouth.

Charon laughed. 'It's all right,' she said. 'I guessed she'd tell you but I honestly don't think it's anything like that. He's sorry for me and . . .'

'A likely story.'

'No, seriously, he told me he was here on business and to clear up a few matters . . .'

'There you are . . .' Aunt Irene said happily. 'You're one of the "few matters". Now what have you got to wear? Absolutely nothing. We must go shopping at once . . .'

'But please . . .' Charon began but Aunt Irene was too excited to listen and actually

Charon admitted to herself it was one of the most exciting moments of her life as they rushed from shop to shop in Durban, trying on clothes and with Aunt Irene shaking her head.

'No, that's not you . . .' she kept saying.

Finally, they found a heavy cream silk frock with fringes. Aunt Irene sighed.

'That's it . . .'

Charon turned round in front of the glass. It certainly made her look terrifically sophisticated. Aunt Irene also bought a gorgeous cyclamen silk cloak and shoes to match and a handbag, then she whisked Charon into a hairdressing salon and had her hair 'heat-combed', then back to the flat and a long soak in a fragrant hot bath and then the ceremony of dressing and parading up and down in front of Aunt Irene.

'I feel rather like a slave about to be sold,' Charon laughed uneasily.

'Nonsense, darling. This could be the most important day of your life,' Aunt Irene said gaily. 'After you're gone, I really must ring Eleanor. She'll be thrilled to bits . . .'

Charon hesitated. 'Please . . . please don't build it up too much, Aunt Irene,' she said imploringly. 'I'm sure there's nothing in it.'

Aunt Irene laughed happily. 'I'm sure there is, but even if there isn't I've had a wonderful time. Have you?'

Charon hugged her for a moment. It was funny, Charon thought, how much more easy it was nowadays to show her love for someone. Oh, how fortunate she was, how very very lucky. Where before she had 'belonged' to no one, now so many people loved her.

'An absolutely heavenly time,' Charon said and the front door bell rang.

Charon was suddenly terrified. Supposing he looked into her eyes and saw the truth? If he guessed, how terribly embarrassed he'd be.

The African maid answered the door and as Charon stiffened, anxious as to what Aunt Irene might say, she heard the door leading to the dining-room close softly and knew Aunt Irene had discreetly disappeared.

Adam came into the room and stood still in the doorway, staring at her.

'Why, Charon,' he said slowly. 'You look different.'

She tried to laugh. 'So everyone tells me. Maybe I'm just growing-up.'

'Growing?' he echoed, his voice dry. 'I'd say, grown up. Ready?'

'Yes.' She let him put the lovely silk cloak over her shoulders, picked up her handbag that matched her shoes and cloak, and they left the flat and down in the lift.

It was a pleasant evening. A very pleasant evening, Charon kept telling herself, but . . . They danced well together to their mutual surprise and she loved every moment of it in his arms, her eyes closed tightly, but then when they sat down, the dull feeling of disappointment returned. Maybe it was because Aunt Irene had made such a thing out of the outing. Adam was his usual friendly self, telling her the local gossip, saying he, too, had been up to the Convent and the Clinic, that he didn't know how long he could stay in Durban but . . . It seemed to Charon there were too many 'buts'. She should have enjoyed the whole evening but she didn't for there were the long dull moments when they talked as they had always talked. Nothing had changed, she felt sure of that. If only she could be like Robin and realise that these things were part of growing-up.

At last the evening was over. In a way, Charon was glad, in another way sad. He helped her into the car and smiled at her.

'Lovely evening,' he said casually.

'Yes, isn't it,' she said but for all she saw of the black sky with its brilliantly shining stars, it might have been raining. She couldn't wait for the sanctuary of her bedroom and the tears she would shed. Why did loving a person have to hurt so much, she wondered.

She was startled when she realised he was driving inland.

'This isn't the way . . .'

He smiled down at her. 'I know. It's early and such a beautiful night, I thought we might take the chance to have a look at the sea. Up the coast, that is. I hate the Parade.'

'So do I. I like it where there are small

coves.'

He nodded. 'I have such a cove in mind.'

He drove silently through the brightly lighted town, turning left and going out down the coast. Finally he parked the car by the side of a railing. The sea was racing in over the light sand. Theirs was the only car there. There was a big hotel, its windows shining, and several houses but not a person in sight.

They walked over the soft sand, Adam carrying Charon's shoes. They didn't talk and the silence seemed to go on for ever. Charon tried to think of something to say but she couldn't.

She was startled when suddenly Adam flung her shoes down and grabbed her hands, holding them tightly. A shiver went through her and she could only hope he didn't notice.

'Charon,' he said abuptly. 'Mum told me to play this quietly but I can't. I know it's impatient of me and we hardly know one another but . . . I feel I've always known you. Charon, I'm doing this very badly but I love you. Is there any hope that in time . . . ?'

She looked at him and perhaps in the moonlight he saw the expression in her eyes for suddenly she was in his arms. She linked her hands behind his neck and closed her eyes as he kissed her.

He still held her but pulled away a little. You love me?' he asked, in a startled voice.

'Yes, Adam, I love you,' she said very slowly.

How wonderful it sounded. 'I can't believe that you love me.'

'But I do. I didn't realise it either until . . .'

'Until?' she urged.

He shrugged. 'I don't know. I think maybe when we went to Joko and you were so brave . . . No, I think I really knew it when I rang you up and Eleanor said you'd gone away. I felt awful. Just as if everything had collapsed. As soon as I could arrange leave, I came down and here I am . . . Now what are you laughing at?' he demanded.

'Am I laughing? Oh, yes, of course I am. It's just because I'm so happy, Adam. So terribly happy . . .' She held his hand against her cheek. 'So many things have happened to me, Adam darling. I can't realise it. There was I, so sorry for myself because I belonged to no one and now . . .'

'You belong to me,' he told her firmly. 'Always remember that. I'll share a bit of you with the others but you're really mine.'

'Adam,' Charon pulled his head down and kissed him gently. 'I couldn't be anyone else's—ever!'